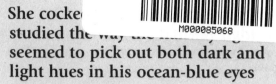

She cocke... studied the ... seemed to pick out both dark and light hues in his ocean-blue eyes

"Can I ask you a question?"

"Shoot."

"Why do my wishes mean so much to you?"

For a moment she didn't think he was going to respond. But finally he did, the words coming hesitantly as he looked into her eyes. "Because *you* do."

She closed her eyes momentarily as Rory's hands moved to her face, the feel of his skin against hers setting off a slew of emotions she wasn't ready to analyze. Not yet, anyway.

"Maggie, I can't stop thinking about y—"

Rising up on tiptoes, she thwarted the rest of his sentence with a kiss.

Dear Reader,

Have you ever received an unexpected gift that resonated with you in a way you can't quite explain?

I have. And just like my main character, Maggie Monroe, mine, too, was a wishing ball.

I remember the day it arrived. I remember the curiosity I felt as I unwrapped the paper and opened the box, not sure what to expect. And I remember the excitement I felt—and still do—at the notion of unleashing a wish into the world and then revisiting it a year later to see if it had come true.

For Maggie, the wishing ball ends up being the start of a whole new life. For me, the wishing ball was the seed that grew this book—a story I hope you love reading as much as I enjoyed writing.

Best wishes,

Laura Bradford

Miracle Baby
Laura Bradford

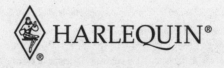

HARLEQUIN®

TORONTO • NEW YORK • LONDON
AMSTERDAM • PARIS • SYDNEY • HAMBURG
STOCKHOLM • ATHENS • TOKYO • MILAN • MADRID
PRAGUE • WARSAW • BUDAPEST • AUCKLAND

Recycling programs
for this product may
not exist in your area.

ISBN-13: 978-0-373-75336-9

MIRACLE BABY

Copyright © 2010 by Laura Bradford

ABOUT THE AUTHOR

Since the age of ten, Laura Bradford hasn't wanted to do anything other than write—news articles, feature stories, business copy and whatever else she could come up with to pay the bills. But they were always diversions from the one thing she wanted to write most—fiction.

Today, with an Agatha Award nomination under her belt and a new mystery series with Berkley Prime Crime, Laura is thrilled to have crossed into the romance genre with her all-time favorite series, Harlequin American Romance.

When she's not writing, Laura enjoys reading, hiking, traveling and all things chocolate. She lives in New York with her two daughters. To contact her, visit her website, www.laurabradford.com.

Books by Laura Bradford

HARLEQUIN AMERICAN ROMANCE

For Jacky…
You couldn't have picked a more perfect gift.

Chapter One

Maggie Monroe reached into the packing box and blindly felt around, seeking the next in a dwindling pile of tissue-wrapped links to her husband and daughter. Precious keepsakes that had been lovingly packed away less than a year earlier, when her life was everything it would never be again.

Swiping the back of her free hand across her eyes, Maggie pulled the telltale mound from the box. For nearly an hour she'd been searching for this particular ornament, panicked at the thought it may have been lost. Yet now that she was sure she'd found it, she couldn't bear to unwrap it, to see the name engraved in cursive across the sterling-silver cradle.

Natalie Renee.

She closed her eyes against the memory that seeped into her heart, tears streaming down her face once again. Every moment of their first Christmas together was etched in her mind—from Natalie's cherubic face in the glow of the colorful lights, to the way Maggie and Jack had deliberately saved a spot in the middle of the tree for their daughter's first ornament. Maggie could still hear his happy sigh when she'd pulled her hand back and smiled triumphantly over her shoulder at the camera, a moment in their too-short life together captured by its lens.

But the sigh she heard in her mind wasn't real. It was simply one of a long line of memories that assailed her day and night, gathering the various pieces of her heart in hope, then shattering them with the dawn of reality....

Jack was gone.

And so was Natalie.

The only thing that remained was the pain of each new day Maggie had to live without them.

Holding the still-wrapped ornament to her chest, she looked up at the bare tree, her vision hampered by tears.

You can do this, Maggie.

"No, I can't," she whispered fiercely before regret hushed her. It was one thing to grieve, quite another to roll over and quit. And while she'd always considered herself strong, fate was showing her otherwise.

She shook her head and focused on the ornaments laid across the floor. So many of them were tied to special moments in her life. Did she really want them packed away in a box?

"You can do this, Maggie," she murmured, willing her heart to heed the words. "You can do this."

A knock at the door caught her by surprise and she turned her clouded gaze toward the sound. For a moment she considered ignoring it and waiting for whoever was on the other side to simply give up and leave her alone, as so many others had in the months following the accident.

But she'd prevailed upon her uncle to give her a room in his inn so she could move forward. Answering the door would be another step.

After swiping at her eyes one last time, Maggie pushed herself off the hardwood and wandered to the door to open it.

"Can I help you?" She knew her voice was raspy, her words broken, but it was the best she could do at the moment. Habits born in sorrow were hard to break overnight.

"Ms. Monroe?"

"Mrs.," she corrected around the sudden lump that sprang up in her throat. Slowly, Maggie began to focus, sucking in a breath at the sight of the handsome man standing in front of her.

A good two inches taller than Jack, the stranger towered over her five-foot-five frame as he raked a strong thick hand through his endearingly disheveled crop of dark brown hair. Unlike her husband, who had seemed at home in button-down shirts and ties, the man standing in front of her wore his pale gray sweatshirt and white-washed denim jeans as if they were a second skin—a skin that pulled taut across his muscled chest and hugged his lower half.

Maggie stepped back, a pang of guilt ripping through her as she hugged Natalie's ornament to her chest, her heart and mind engaged in full-fledged battle. Yes, the man in front of her was handsome; she'd have to be blind not to see that. But the moistening of her hands and the skip of her heartbeat the moment their eyes met was nothing but a figment of her imagination.

"Oh, I'm sorry. Your uncle said you'd be living here alone. So I just assumed you were sing—"

"You know my uncle?" she interrupted, in an effort to keep him from finishing his sentence. This familiarity was too much, too soon. She needed baby steps first.

"Of course." The man thrust out his hand. "I'm Rory O'Brien."

Rory?

The name rang a bell but she was at a loss. A whoosh of white noise filled her ears as she stared at his out-stretched hand waiting for hers….

"I'm sorry, should I know you?"

A hearty laugh bubbled up from somewhere inside the man's soul, a sound that first intrigued and then sickened her. "I'm the carpenter your uncle hired to restore the inn in his absence."

"Carpenter? Oh. Oh, yes, I'm sorry." Shaking her head against the ludicrous notion she'd felt something for this stranger, Maggie placed her hand in his. "Uncle Doug told me about you. He said if anyone could restore Lake Shire Inn to the way it was in my childhood it would be you."

"You came here when you were a kid?"

"Oh, yes…" She leaned against the door frame as she traveled to a place she'd sought many times over the past eleven months—a place where she'd felt happy and strong. She hoped desperately to find those feelings once again. "It was nothing short of magical."

"Magical, huh?"

"To me it was." She met his eyes for the first time and was rewarded by the appearance of dimples, carved into his cheeks. "Do you really think you can restore this place to what it once was?"

"That's my intention."

"All fifteen rooms?"

"Well, I don't think your uncle would take kindly to me only doing fourteen of them, do you?"

"I guess not."

Rory grinned. "Don't mind me. That was my attempt at being funny."

The heat that shot through every nook and cranny of Maggie's body reminded her that their hands were still joined. She yanked hers back as a wave of nausea racked her. "I'm sorry, I don't feel very well today. I need to go."

"Wait!" Thrusting his work boot against the base of the closing door, Rory waved a small wrapped box in the air. "Your uncle asked me to give this to you. He told me to make sure I got it to you *today*. He wanted you to have it while you were dec—"

Rory's eyes left her face and went to the unwrapped ornaments spread beneath the stark, naked tree she'd promised herself she'd decorate.

"My mom used to do that. You know, set all the ornaments out first and then hang them."

But how could she decorate it? Then she'd be making new memories....

Rory's voice broke through her thoughts. "My friends all did it one at a time—you know, not so organized. They'd unwrap one and then hang it. Unwrap one and hang it. Uh, Mrs. Monroe? Are you okay?"

Forcing her attention on the here and now, Maggie

shrugged. "I'm not sure what okay is anymore. It's certainly nothing like it used to be." As he once more looked into her face, she forced the corners of her mouth upward in an effort to chase the worry from his sky-blue eyes, which seemed as if they should sparkle, not fret. "Could you just call me Maggie? I think that would be best. Part of that first step and all."

"First step?" When she didn't respond, he moved on. "Maggie, huh? That's a beautiful name. Suits you real well." Rory looked down at the carefully wrapped gift box and held it out to her. "Your uncle has been really good to me. In fact, if it weren't for him giving me this position, I'd probably be looking through the classifieds for another desk job. So please, take this."

Squaring her shoulders, she reached out, took the box.

"He said you were to open it right away."

"Why?"

"I don't know. My guess is it has something to do with your decorating."

She glanced down at the gift. "It's something new for the tree, isn't it?"

Rory's shoulders hitched upward, only to fall back down once again. "I don't know. But new is good, isn't it?"

She shrugged. "I—I just can't hang it right now."

"Do you need hooks? I can run home and get some. It won't take but a minute or two."

"No!" Realizing her voice was sharper than she'd intended, she offered a quick apology. "I have hooks. Plenty of them."

Rory gestured toward the pile of brightly colored objects on the floor. "Afraid you have too many?"

She shook her head, loosening her grip on the ornament still clasped to her chest. "No, it's not that. It's just—well, it's just that I'm trying, I really am, but it's hard. Harder than I thought it would be."

Silence blanketed the cozy, wood-paneled suite as she focused on the tissue-wrapped mound in her left hand and the brightly wrapped package in her right. She knew he was watching her, but it didn't matter. She was at a loss over what to say or do at that moment, not to mention the rest of her life.

Finally he spoke, his deep voice surprisingly soft. "Maybe there's a reason your uncle wanted you to have this package today. Maybe he knew it was going to be hard. Maybe whatever's in this box is meant to help somehow."

"I'm not sure how it can. How anything ever can," she mumbled, her words barely audible to her own ears. "I'm trying every day, but it's not working."

"Maybe I could help." Reaching out, Rory touched the mound in her left hand. "Why don't you let me hold that so you can open your present?"

She jumped back, grasping Natalie's first Christmas ornament in a death grip.

He retracted his arm in a flash and raised his hands, palms outward. "I'm sorry, I didn't mean anything. I was just trying to help. Look…I can see this is a bad time." He took a step toward the door. "I'm sorry I barged in. I didn't mean to cause you any trouble. I'll leave you alone now."

Alone.

Again.

"Wait," she whispered, her voice shaking along with her hands. "Please. Don't go."

HAD SHE NOT REPEATED HER plea, he would have chalked it up to his mind playing tricks—wishing for something that simply wasn't going to happen.

But she had.

Turning around, Rory studied the woman who looked at him with red-rimmed eyes. Maggie Monroe was beautiful by anyone's standards. Her soft brown hair cascaded across her shoulders and halfway down her back in natural waves that emphasized her high cheekbones and plump, kissable lips. Her eyelashes, wet with tears, framed dark brown eyes that vacillated between looking at the floor and peering up at him. The vulnerability and deep-rooted sadness they displayed tugged at his heart.

He looked from her face to her body, noting how the off-white cowl-neck sweater and baggy jeans nearly swallowed her whole.

"Could you stay? For just a little while?"

"Are you sure? I don't want to impose." And he didn't. Yet there was something about this woman that spoke to him on a level he'd never experienced before. Maybe it was simply the carpenter in him coming out—some inbred desire to fix things that were obviously broken. Maybe it was the fact that this woman's uncle had come along at a low point in Rory's life and made an offer that had given him the kick he needed. Or maybe it was the overwhelming desire to kiss away her tears….

Maggie thrust the small square package back into his hand. "Could you open it for me?"

He stared down at the box, then at her. "You want me to open it? Why?"

Her shoulders rose and fell beneath her cavernous sweater. "I don't know. I just think taking half a step is better than no step right now."

Cautiously, he met her eyes, his curiosity rising. Whatever was wrong with this woman, it was obviously something major. Too many questions might be more than she could handle, so he settled on one.

"You sure?" he asked. "Sometimes opening a gift makes you feel good."

"Not today." Maggie gestured toward the navy blue couch that sat at an angle to the stone fireplace. Despite the below-freezing temperatures of the winds blowing off Lake Shire, the wood he'd stacked in preparation for her arrival sat untouched.

"I can light a fire for you if you'd like. Winters around here are mighty rough."

"They certainly are. In fact, I remember a few winters when the fireplace was the only thing that kept me from turning into a human ice cube." A hint of longing sprang into her eyes, only to disappear just as quickly. "I couldn't ask you to make a fire. Really, I'm—"

Setting her uncle's package on the end table beside the couch, Rory pushed the sleeves of his sweatshirt up his arms. "You didn't ask. I offered."

"But I—"

"No arguments. Your uncle would have my hide if I sensed you were cold and I didn't do something to help."

A tiny laugh escaped Maggie's throat, a welcome sound that grabbed hold of his heart.

"I can see you know my uncle well." After nodding toward the kitchenette on the other side of the wall, she cocked her head. "I haven't stopped at the market yet, but I could get you a glass of water."

"That would be great, thanks." He watched as she set the tissue-wrapped mound on the table beside her uncle's gift, his throat constricting at the sadness in her face. "I promise I'll have this fire going before you get back."

Without a word, Maggie Monroe headed toward the kitchen, her petite frame disappearing around the corner as he glanced toward the tissue paper and shifted from foot to foot.

He knew it was none of his business. Knew he should just do what he'd promised. But his curiosity was kicking into overdrive. Doug Rigsby's niece was hurting deep inside her soul. One had only to look at her eyes to unearth that fact.

Her reaction to his initial greeting was simply icing on the cake.

But if she was married, as she'd implied, where was the guy? And why had Doug made a point of saying his niece would be living there alone?

Rory heard a cabinet door open and knew his window of opportunity was rapidly closing. The key to Maggie Monroe's sadness was inside that tissue paper. He was sure of it.

The sound of ice cubes clanking into glasses propelled him forward, the drive to understand Maggie Monroe overriding the voice in his head that chided him for being sneaky. And dishonest.

Carefully, he unwrapped the first layer of paper, and then a second, the overhead light glinting off the silver object inside. Slowly, gently, Rory lifted the ornament from the tissue, his eyes glued to the delicate silver cradle with an infant's tiny form tucked beneath a silver blanket. A sash across the blanket was inscribed with delicate cursive engraving.

Natalie Renee.

The faucet turned off and he froze in response.

"Would you like something to eat?" Maggie called out. "I have some cookies."

"Uh…yeah, sure. Um, cookies sound good." Rory quickly rewrapped the ornament in the crinkled paper, his hurried and guilt-ridden efforts resulting in a package that bore little resemblance to its earlier form.

He tried again, his second attempt more successful than the first. Stepping back, he breathed a sigh of relief. He shouldn't have peeked. But he couldn't help himself. He wanted to find a way to help Maggie—to banish the pain from her eyes.

Raking his fingers through his hair, he turned toward the fireplace and the kindling he'd placed in the iron bin beside the hearth just three days earlier. With a practiced hand, he set about the task of lighting the fire as he pondered the meaning behind the ornament.

Did Maggie have a daughter? And if so, where was

she? Had her husband kidnapped the child during some sort of custody battle?

Rory snapped a thick stick in two as a flash of anger coursed through his body. What kind of idiot would want to hurt a woman in that way?

Maggie's footsteps startled him. "Hey, there. I'm almost done here. I just need to light it." He grabbed the box of tall matches he'd set beside the bin, and struck one against the side. "And there we go!"

He glanced over his shoulder, watched the reflection of the fire in her eyes and felt his chest tighten in response. There were no two ways about it. Maggie Monroe was gorgeous, tear-swollen face and all.

Rising to his feet, he gestured toward the fireplace. "You like?"

"I like," she repeated softly. Pulling her focus from the flames, she held out a glass. "Here's your water."

"Maggie, what the hell happened?" He grabbed her forearm as the sleeve of her sweater slid back to reveal an angry red scar that started just above her wrist and traveled up her arm.

She shoved the glass into his free hand and pulled down her sleeve. "It's nothing. Forget it."

Setting the glass on the mantel behind him, Rory grasped her hand and gently pushed her sleeve upward again. "This is far from nothing." He met her pained gaze with his own, felt the longing to pull her into his arms. Instead, he simply asked the question burning in his heart. "Are you okay?"

He watched as she nibbled her lower lip, noting the tears that hovered in the corners of her eyes. Finally she spoke, her voice little more than a whisper. "I'm alive. Only I'm not sure how to live anymore."

Without thinking, he reached out, pulled the fragile woman toward him and held her tight as he sensed her fleeting resistance. For several long moments he simply cradled her as she sobbed against his chest. More than anything he wanted to guide her face upward, to wipe away the tears he felt soaking through his sweatshirt. But he didn't want to scare her.

And somehow he knew a gesture like that would.

Whatever Maggie Monroe had experienced, it explained the vulnerability he'd sensed from the moment she'd opened the door. What explained the *fear* she exhibited as she suddenly pulled away from him, though, was anyone's guess.

"I—I need you to leave."

He felt his shoulders slump at her words, their definitiveness crystal clear. He'd overstepped his bounds.

"Maggie, I'm sorry. I didn't mean any harm, I really didn't. It's just that I saw that scar…and the pain in your eyes…and I wanted to make it go away." Rory knew he was blabbering, but he didn't care. He needed to make her understand. To make her see he only wanted to help.

"I want it to go away, too. But if that happens, I'm afraid I'll lose them forever," she whispered as she stared at the fire roaring behind him, the flames flickering in her deadened eyes.

Chapter Two

Driven from her bed before dawn by nightmares, Maggie stepped into the bathroom and pulled on the plush, baby-pink robe Jack had given her for her last birthday. Curve-hugging at the time, the garment now looked as if it had been purchased for someone a good thirty pounds heavier.

She leaned against the shiny white pedestal sink and peered into the mirror, the unfamiliar face it reflected startling a gasp from her throat. Sure, she'd lost some weight; her clothes told that story. But when had her eyes taken on that haunted quality? When had her cheeks drawn in so dramatically as to make her look malnourished?

Ten months, twenty-two days and eight hours ago. That's when...

Shaking her head against the memories of that icy January night, she forced herself to focus on the face that no longer looked like the Maggie Monroe she had been last Christmas.

What would Jack say if he could see her now?

Maggie, you need to eat. You need to take care of yourself.

She smiled at the memory of his voice, inhaled the delicious sense of certainty with which her heart had formed his answer—reactions that were chased away just as quickly by the next question that came to her mind: *How would Natalie react if she saw me now?*

She'd be scared....

Sucking in her breath at the realization, Maggie squared her shoulders and studied her face more closely. The circles beneath her eyes were dark, but nothing a little foundation couldn't mask. And the hollow look to her cheeks—well, she could work on that a little at a time, starting with something that resembled a real meal. Like maybe an apple *and* a muffin.

But first she had to make an apology.

Padding back into her room, Maggie yanked open the top drawer of the mahogany dresser, a glance at the room's lone window confirming what she already knew to be true—winter had set its sights on the shores of Lake Shire. The frost on the glass added the exclamation point.

She rummaged through the clothes she'd pulled from her suitcases less than forty-eight hours earlier. So many of her things were gifts from well-meaning friends who'd been grasping at straws to make her smile in the year since the accident. While their efforts were touching, no one had ever seemed to understand her need to hold on to what was familiar.

A need that was as strong today as ever. The only way she could make the face in the mirror look like Maggie

Monroe again was to *be her* through and through—
clothes, appetite, exercise, books, crafts….

Natalie and Jack...

The familiar lump sprang into her throat as Maggie
grabbed hold of a ruby-red sweater and a pair of old jeans
that had been one of her favorite outfits. The fact that the
sweater now hung on her and the jeans threatened to slip
off her hips was beside the point. Belts had their place.

Returning to the bathroom, Maggie ran a brush
through her hair, pulling the wavy cascade into a high
ponytail that softened the unfamiliar lines in her face.
She peered into the mirror, pleased with the slight im-
provement.

Did she look good? No. But at least she didn't look
as if home was a cardboard box underneath a bridge
in some overpopulated city. And besides, she was just
leaving her suite long enough to offer an apology and to
open a gift.

She steered her gaze away from the still-bare tree in
the middle of the living room as she strode toward the
door, well aware of the fact that she'd let *them* down. She
had quit once again, defeated by a mountain that seemed
too high to climb.

But not today. Today she would take steps. Real
steps.

With a long, deliberate inhale, Maggie swooped up
the brightly wrapped package from the end table where
she'd left it and yanked open the door.

The firm tap of a hammer came from somewhere off
to her left. She turned in that direction, her heart thud-

ding in her chest at the thought of coming face-to-face
with Rory O'Brien once again.

What was it about him that made her so nervous? Was
it the way he'd grabbed her arm when he'd spotted the
scar? The way he'd repeatedly insisted she open a gift
she couldn't bear to unwrap, innocently prodding for an
explanation she didn't want to give?

It wasn't nerves. It was attraction....

She paused in the middle of the hallway and covered
her mouth with her free hand. But it was too late. The un-
spoken words had hit their mark. Only they were wrong.
They had to be.

Tightening her grip on the package, Maggie clenched
her teeth in defiance as she forced her feet to keep
moving. She'd been uncomfortable with a stranger seeing
her pain, that was all. The notion that it might be anything resembling attraction was nothing short of crazy.
Her heart would forever belong to Jack and Natalie.

The hammering stopped, only to start again, the sound
coming from a room less than ten feet away.

You can do this, Maggie. It's just an apology.

"It's just an apology, that's all," she repeated to herself
in a whisper.

Stopping outside the open doorway, she peeked inside.
There, on the other side of the gutted room, was Rory,
poised atop a ladder in the back corner. For a moment she
simply watched him, her eyes focused on his muscular
arms as he worked, her body revisiting the warmth and
feel of their compassionate embrace.

Banishing the ridiculous memory, Maggie knocked
on the door frame, determined to do what she'd come

to do despite her sudden sense of guilt and the resurrected fluttering in her stomach. "Rory? Do you have a minute?"

The hammering ceased as he glanced in her direction. A slow smile spread across his face, lighting his eyes, and she swallowed.

"Well, isn't this a pleasant surprise." Resting the hammer on the top step of the ladder, he climbed down, wiping his hands against his jeans when he reached the floor. "Are you feeling any better this morning?"

She attempted a smile and shrugged. "I wanted to apologize for my behavior last night. I never should have subjected you to my emotions the way I did. Especially when you were simply carrying out a favor my uncle asked of you."

Rory stopped just inches from where she stood, his gaze traveling slowly down her body, only to return to her face with a look that made her swallow once again. "Please, no apology. We can't help what we feel and when we feel it. I'm just sorry I pushed the package the way I did."

"It's okay." She held out the gift box. "If it meant enough to my uncle to have you track me down, the least I can do is open it, right?"

A dimple appeared in Rory's left cheek, then in his right one as his smile widened. "Now you're talking." Glancing around, he threw up his hands. "I'd offer you a place to sit but, as you can see, there's no—wait!"

The moment his hand reached for hers she felt it—an undeniable electrical charge that started at the point of impact and spread throughout her body, destroying the protest that rose in her throat.

"Here. This'll work." Gently releasing her, Rory brushed off the top piece of lumber in a nearby stack. "You can sit right here while you open it."

She looked down, the lingering warmth of his touch bringing tears to her eyes. Shaking off the emotions warring in her heart, she sat where he indicated, her exhale blowing a renegade strand of hair from her face. "Okay. Let's do this."

She slowly unwrapped the package as Rory lowered himself beside her, his thigh brushing hers while yet another wave of warmth spread throughout her body. Forcing her focus onto the square package in her hands, Maggie pushed aside the wrapping paper to reveal a red box.

"Hmm. Well, it's not a bread box," Rory murmured. "And it's probably not a marble, unless your uncle is into trickery."

She laughed, the genuinely happy sound startling her as much as it obviously did Rory. "Trickery?"

He bobbed his head, his eyes sparkling. "Yeah, you know—stick a marble in a box five times its size. Or hand someone an envelope with the key to a new car inside… That kind of thing."

It was hard not to be taken by Rory O'Brien's infectious smile, or the mischievous sparkle that lit his sapphire-blue eyes, or the dimples in his cheeks….

"Have you ever done that? Been tricky with a gift?" she asked, determined to nip her visual inventorying in the bud.

"Nope. But I could see why a person might…if it was for someone special."

She nodded, biting back a smile as she imagined wrapping a wrench or a hammer or whatever kind of tool Rory might need inside a large appliance box.

"C'mon, the suspense is killing me!" His deep voice cut through her woolgathering. "What is it?"

With a shrug, Maggie removed the lid from the box and peered inside, the feel of Rory's breath as he looked over her shoulder sending a tiny shiver down her spine. "I don't know." Looping her index finger through the red satin ribbon on top, she lifted a round silver ball from the box. "Ohhh, it's beautiful."

The polished ornament dangled from her finger, gleaming in the morning light that streamed through a bay window nearby.

Leaning across her lap, Rory held the ball steady with the palm of his hand. "Look, there's something engraved across the center."

Together, they bent closer and read the inscription aloud. "Wishes."

"Wishes?" she repeated as she studied the ball from another angle. "What do you think that means?"

"I don't know."

Maggie handed the silver ball to Rory, dug around inside the box and extracted a small white envelope with tiny strips of blank paper inside. Holding one up, she shrugged again. "What do you think this is for?"

"I have no idea, unless…" His voice trailed off as he studied the ornament more closely. "Hey, wait, I think it opens." She watched as he gently twisted the bottom half from the top. Sure enough, the ball opened to reveal a red velvet interior. "That's kinda cool, don't you think? Though what it's for I have no—wait!"

He pointed at the strips of paper. "I get it now. You write your wishes there and put them inside. Then you open it next Christmas and see how many of them came true."

Maggie stared at the ornament, her hands beginning to tremble as Rory's words took root in her heart. It didn't matter how many slips of paper were clutched in her fist. There could be ten, twenty, thirty, for all she cared. It simply didn't matter.

Because when it came to making wishes, there was only one.

ALTHOUGH HER DEMEANOR that morning could never have been described as giddy or carefree, it didn't take a rocket scientist to detect the dark cloud that had passed over Maggie's face at the discovery of the ornament's intent. Nor was it hard to figure out why, even if Rory hadn't gathered all the pieces just yet.

Maggie Monroe was grieving. That much was obvious. What exactly she was grieving over was still a mystery. A mystery that surely explained the scar on her arm, the haunted look in her eyes and the ornament engraved with the name of a child that was nowhere to be found.

But one thing was certain. The beautiful woman sitting beside him had taken a big step by seeking him out—a step he didn't intend to let her undo anytime soon.

He tilted the silver ball back and forth in the light. "You know what's the best part about wishes?"

He glanced at her in time to see her shake her head, her eyes cast downward. Setting the ornament into the box between them, he swiveled his legs to the left, his knee grazing hers. "Wishes don't always have to be about huge things. I mean, sure, it's nice to have a great big wish, but it's also fun to have little ones."

Without waiting for a reply he continued on, determined to banish the sadness from her expression even for just a little while. "Last weekend I found myself wishing for a little fun…something that would put a smile on my face."

He met her gaze with what he hoped was an encouraging smile, anything to get her back out of her shell.

"And?" she whispered.

"And I sprawled out on my couch Saturday night with a bowl of microwave popcorn and a rented movie the salesclerk said was guaranteed to make me laugh."

"Did it?"

Grateful that she was finally talking once again, he nodded, words rushing from his mouth. "Yeah, it did. And it was exactly what I needed at the moment."

"But don't you think these slips of paper—" she raised her hand in the air before letting it fall back to her lap "—are designed for bigger wishes?"

He considered her question. "I suppose. But that doesn't mean you can't have smaller ones, or that they have to be written down and stowed away inside a wishing ball."

Resting her elbows on her thighs, Maggie dropped

her head into her hands with an audible exhale. Her high ponytail fell forward and to the right, blocking his view of her exquisite profile. There were so many things in life he could fix—walls, steps, ceilings, floors, furniture, you name it. But for the second time in his life, Rory felt totally inept.

And it killed him.

Racking his brain for something he could do to help, he settled on the first thing that came to mind—securing more time with Maggie Monroe. He glanced at the window and then his watch as he hatched a workable plan. "I actually have one of those right now."

Slowly, she lifted her head, her dark brown eyes filled with the same confusion he heard in her voice. "Have what?"

"One of those smaller wishes that aren't necessarily meant to be written down but I hope will come true."

"What is it?"

"Breakfast at the diner. I was so hell-bent on getting this room under way that I left my house without so much as a banana. Unfortunately, my stomach is now protesting that decision."

With rapid movements, Maggie dropped the paper strips into the tiny envelope and placed it inside the box with the wishing ball. Sliding the box across the lumber pile in his direction, she stood. "Then I'll let you get to it."

Without realizing what he was doing, he reached out and grasped her arm. "No, please. There's a second part to my wish."

"Second part?"

He felt a surge of longing at the sight of the too-thin, yet beautiful woman standing in front of him with her large woebegone eyes and her plump, sensuous lips. Oh, what he wouldn't give to pull her close and kiss her senseless....

Shaking the inappropriate thoughts from his mind, Rory, too, stood, still holding on to her. "The first part is breakfast at the diner. The second part is to have you accompany me."

A wash of crimson blossomed across her cheeks. "I can't. I—"

"Have you eaten yet?" he asked in a rush, his mind running in circles as he searched for words that wouldn't scare her away.

"No, but—"

"Neither have I."

"But—"

"Look, being a carpenter is great. But doing the kind of work I do means I'm alone all day with no one to talk to but myself. And while I can be scintillating company the vast majority of the time, I could surely stand a little spice in my routine." He ducked his head to the side in an effort to regain eye contact with the woman standing less than a foot away.

After an awkward moment of silence, she finally spoke, her quiet voice sporting a hint of playfulness. "Scintillating, you say?"

He inhaled deeply. "Yup."

"Then I guess you're two for two this week."

"Two for two?" he repeated, his heart completely captivated by the tiny smile he saw flitting across her lips.

"With wishes."

"Ahhh," he said with a laugh. "You're right. And you know something else?"

She shook her head as he grabbed his keys and gestured toward the door. "No, what's that?"

"I could get used to this. *Quickly.*"

Chapter Three

It wasn't long ago she'd prided herself on making smart decisions and having a cool head. But like everything else in her life, that, too, had obviously changed.

Looking across the table at her breakfast companion, Maggie couldn't help the incessant second-guessing that had plagued her from the moment Rory led her to his pickup truck in the parking lot of Lake Shire Inn.

What on earth had she been thinking? She didn't even know him. And what would Jack think of her sharing a meal with another man?

He'd be glad you're eating.

As if on cue, her stomach grumbled, a sound so loud and so long it made the man on the other side of the table laugh.

"Sounds like someone's hungry." Rory tapped the menu in front of him, his smile stretching across his face. "Which is a very good thing, because curing that is Delilah's specialty."

Pushing a wayward strand of hair back toward her ponytail, Maggie cocked her head. "Delilah?"

He nodded as his sapphire eyes inventoried their

surroundings before coming to rest on her face. "Delilah owns this place. She's been in business here for more years than I've been alive. She's changed the interior, the display cases over by the door and even the menu on occasion, but satisfying stomach rumbles? That's been a staple for as long as I can remember."

Maggie looked around at the bench-lined tables that dotted the quaint restaurant. In honor of the season, a tiny table-size tree surrounded by ketchup and mustard containers graced the wide window ledge above each booth.

"Every Christmas season she decorates the place, adding something new. Last year was the themed trees at all the tables." Rory beckoned to a robust woman who appeared to be squinting at them from a far corner. Within seconds, the sixtysomething woman was beside their table, a pad of paper and a pen in her hand.

"Would you look at who's finally decided to grace us with his presence?" Dramatically, the woman placed a hand at the throat of her powder-blue, button-down dress, a look of mock surprise on her gently lined face. "Why, Rory O'Brien, if I hadn't had my vision checked just the other day, I'd think I was seeing things. But Dr. Rinaldi swears I've got the eyesight of a hawk. In fact, he says it's so good I may get through another ten years without needing glasses. So it really must be you sitting here in my booth. Either that or you've got a twin broth—"

The woman clutched the pad to her chest as her cheeks drained of all perceivable color. "Oh, Rory, I'm so sorry. I didn't mean to say—"

Maggie shot a glance across the table, saw the flash

of anguish on Rory's face. It disappeared quickly and he shook the apology aside. "C'mon now, Delilah, I've been in here," he said in a teasing tone.

Seeming to respond on cue, the woman continued the playful banter with a sniff of disagreement. "A week ago, maybe…"

Rory winked at Maggie, all traces of pain gone from his eyes. "Delilah likes to keep tabs on her customers. Miss a day, she'll overlook it. Miss two, she gets a bit cranky. Miss three, and she's convinced you've defected to Larchmont."

"Larchmont?"

"Larchmont is two towns to the east. Where Sam's Diner is located." He leaned across the table, his breath warm on her cheek. "But Sam's got nothing on Delilah. Especially her Belgian waffles."

Maggie's stomach grumbled again.

"My Belgian waffles?" the woman prompted with a raised eyebrow.

"And her eggs Benedict, her pancakes, her French toast and—" he sat back in the booth, lifted the menu from the table and handed it to the owner "—every other item she makes. Today, though, it's her Belgian waffles I'm after."

"That's better." Delilah tucked Rory's menu under her arm and nodded at Maggie. "And how about you, darlin'? What can I get you?"

Maggie skimmed the menu, to no avail. She simply couldn't focus. Couldn't wrap her mind around the notion of eating an actual meal. "I don't know. I can't recall the last time I ate anything besides an apple…." Her voice trailed off as she looked from Rory to Delilah and back again, their raised eyebrows proof positive she'd spoken the words aloud. "Um, I'll have a waffle, too."

The woman poised her pen above the pad. "How about I have the cook make you a half-size order?"

"Half-size?"

Not unkindly, Delilah nodded. "Rory, here, has an insatiable appetite. Where he puts it is anyone's guess. But if you're not used to eating, it's best to take it slow. You know, let your body build back up again."

"That sounds good." When Delilah turned toward the kitchen, Maggie sank back against the booth's vinyl cushion. "I think you should have asked for a job description from my uncle *before* you agreed to renovate the inn."

His eyebrows furrowed. "Why?"

She fiddled with the flatware on the paper mat and shrugged. "Because I imagine babysitting isn't something carpenters often find themselves doing."

"Babysitting?"

"Yeah, like you're doing right now. With me." Maggie released the fork and continued on folding her paper napkin. "My uncle can be a little transparent at times."

Rory shook his head and reached across the table for her hand. "Your uncle has absolutely nothing to do with us having breakfast together."

She leveled a look of disbelief in his direction as she pulled her fingers out of reach. "C'mon. I've known my uncle my whole life and I know all about his sweet—albeit meddling—streak. I know he put you up to this."

Again Rory shook his head. "No. All he told me was

that you'd be arriving the day after Thanksgiving and that you'd be staying in his suite during the renovations. He told me I might not see much of you and that I should try to keep the noise to a minimum when possible."

"You're supposed to renovate quietly?" She propped her elbows on the edge of the table. "Please don't let my being at the inn affect your work. Really, I can handle the sound of hammering and drilling. It's the sounds I replay in my head that—"

She threw her shoulders back, causing her ponytail to sway against her neck. "Look, just do whatever work you need to do and don't worry about me."

"That's a mighty tall order when you look so sad."

She shrugged, the desire to talk to someone virtually overpowering. The fact that this particular someone was handsome and kind only made it—

Don't go there!

Shaking off the memory of his warm arms wrapped around her as she sobbed through the pain of finding Natalie's ornament, Maggie met his pointed gaze with her own, determined not to be lulled into a conversation that would only result in tears. "You mean like you just did five minutes ago when that woman mentioned a twin brother?"

The second the words were out of her mouth she regretted them—regretted the hurt that momentarily dulled the sparkle in his eyes. She held her palms up. "I'm sorry, I shouldn't have said that. I know what it is to feel pain and I know what it means to want to hold it close."

"Then you also know about the damage that can be

caused by holding it close, yes?" Rory swiped a hand through his hair.

"Damage? I don't see that. It's—"

Delilah stopped beside their table and smiled at Maggie. "I swear I'm losing my mind. I forgot to get your drink order, hon."

"Um, a glass of milk sounds good, I guess."

"Milk it is."

Rory reached out and grabbed hold of her arm. "Delilah, wait. I want you to meet Maggie. Maggie Monroe. She's staying at the inn."

Delilah's brows furrowed. "I thought Doug had closed for business during the renovation work."

"He did. But Maggie is his niece."

A smile lit the woman's eyes as she leaned in for a closer look. "Maggie? Little Maggie Rigsby?"

She couldn't help but laugh. "I—I guess. Though no one has called me that in a while."

Delilah clapped her hands together. "I remember when you were no higher than my knee." The woman met Rory's eyes and pointed to Maggie. "This little one was the shyest thing I'd ever seen. Hardly said boo. Her uncle would have to practically peel her off his leg on the rare occasion they came in for dinner."

Maggie remembered it well. Even though it was a lifetime ago.

"You don't remember Delilah?" Rory asked. "Or this diner?"

"I only remember bits and pieces of that time."

"You remember the fires that kept you warm."

"Because that was one of the only things that took

away the chill." She shifted and smiled up at Delilah. "Actually, instead of the milk…could I have a hot chocolate?"

"Coming right up." The woman took one last look at her before heading off to fill the order.

"Wow. It's not often I see Delilah like that."

"Like what?"

"Surprised." Rory leaned forward. "Delilah knows this town inside out and backward."

Maggie shrugged. "I don't know what to say to that."

He laughed. "So tell me…what made the inn so magical to a shy little girl?"

Tracing the lines of the Formica table, she considered Rory's question and found the answer suddenly crystal clear. "It was safe. And it was warm. And it was happy."

His left eyebrow rose. "Safe?"

"My parents were killed when I was five. One day I was a normal kindergartner with a mommy and a daddy, and the next I was living with an aunt who had six kids of her own."

For a moment he simply studied her, his expression morphing into one she knew all too well. But for once, the pity didn't translate into the same anticlimactic apology she'd heard all her life. "Wow. That had to be rough."

"It was. At times. My mom's sister tried, though, she really did. It wasn't her fault I slipped between the cracks. That probably happens in most large families anyway. But I'd gone from being an only child who adored her parents to being one of seven in a family that wasn't really mine."

"I didn't realize your uncle was married. Or that he had kids."

She shook her head. "He didn't. Uncle Doug is my dad's brother. I got to visit him once a year. Most of the visits were to the inn during the summer, when the tourist season was in full swing. He'd turn the reins over to his office manager and spend the entire week with me. We'd set off in his boat early in the morning and not come back until dusk, his bucket filled with fish and my face aching from all the laughter. One time, maybe twice, I got to visit in the winter. And as much as I loved our time on the lake in the summer, I loved having the inn all to ourselves in the winter. Because then it was just us."

"And lots of fires in the fireplace?"

"And lots of fires in the fireplace," she echoed. "It was during my visits here that I finally found *me*. A me that had more courage and strength than I realized at the time."

He leaned back as Delilah approached with their breakfast. "Sounds like you found hope, too."

"Hope," she repeated in a whisper. "I hadn't really thought of it that way, but yeah...I found hope."

"Soup's on." Delilah lowered the tray of food to the edge of their table, divvying up their order with grace and speed. "Full order for you—" she plunked Rory's Belgian waffle on the table in front of him "—and a half-size order for you."

Maggie peered down at the plate and the waffle nearly spilling over the sides. "This is a half-size order?"

Plunking yet another waffle in front of Rory, Delilah nodded. "It sure is." She lifted the tray and tucked it under her arm. "You kids need anything else you just holler, y'hear?"

Maggie stared at the food in front of her, her stomach performing a simultaneous grumble and flip. "I can't eat all this."

"Eat what you can." Rory grabbed a miniature silver pitcher from beneath the table's small Christmas tree and handed it to her, the high-wattage sparkle of earlier returning to his eyes. "Can't eat a waffle without syrup. It's the best part."

Fifteen minutes later Maggie pointed at her half-empty plate. "Do you know this is the first real meal I've had in…" She thought for a moment. "Well, let's just say it's been a long time."

A satisfied grin crept across his face. "And do you know this is the first time I've had a conversation with my meal in aeons? I mean, I love carpentry, I really do. In fact, I couldn't imagine doing anything else. But the nature of the restorations I do has me working by myself ninety-nine percent of the time."

"And the other one percent?" she asked.

"That's just the two or three words exchanged with whatever delivery guy's brought the lumber or special-ized tool I need for a particular project."

"Surely you talk to more people than that, right?"

His shoulders rose and fell with a lazy shrug. "Not really."

"What about your—" she glanced at his left hand,

noting that his ring finger was bare "—girlfriend? Parents? Siblings? Friends?"

She watched as he chased a bite of waffle around his syrup-soaked plate with a fork. "I'm not involved with anyone at the moment, haven't been for a while. My mom passed on two and a half years ago, my father shortly after my—" He stopped, cleared his throat and shifted in his seat before diving back into the conversation in a slightly different place. "As for friends, well, I guess I had some at one time."

"At one time?"

He nodded. "I pushed them away."

"Ahhh, yes. I know it well."

If he was curious about her statement, though, he let it pass. And she was glad. Despite the fact that they'd danced around two potentially heavy topics prior to the arrival of their food, breakfast with Rory had been surprisingly comfortable.

Maybe even a little fun.

The last thing she wanted was for that to change. Not now, anyway.

"So, as you can see, having breakfast with you has nothing to do with babysitting and everything to do with my own selfish motives."

"And wishes?" she teased, as a burst of warmth spread throughout her body at his welcomed reassurance.

Dimples formed in his cheeks as he met her eyes across the table. "And wishes."

"You wanna know something?" The question surprised her as it left her mouth.

"Absolutely."

"I'm not sure it was an actual wish. It was really more of a promise to myself…but just this morning, before I came down to apologize, I made a pact with myself to eat something real for breakfast. And—" she gestured at her plate "—I did."

He studied her intently, an act she was surprised to realize didn't bother her at all. When he finally spoke, his voice was gentle. "It's like I said. A wish doesn't always have to be a monumental, life-changing thing. It can be something small, something simple. The key is appreciating it when it comes true."

Unable to think of what to say, she simply nodded.

He pointed at his chest and continued, his strong voice almost melodic to her ears. "I know it's probably hard to imagine, but I used to wear a tie to work. My wish, though, was to work with my hands. There was something about returning things to their original beauty that called to me when I wasn't much more than twelve."

"I like to make things," Maggie blurted, shocked by the admission. Sure, she'd always liked crafts and making things to brighten a home, but to say it out loud?

"Like what?"

"I don't know. It's probably silly."

"Making things with your hands doesn't sound silly to me."

"Well, I can make seasonal wall hangings…and I've toyed with personalizing picture frames—you know, for special occasions." She leaned her head against the booth, the once familiar tug of a smile lifting her mouth. "I've even sold some of my things at a few craft shows over the years."

"Ever think about opening an actual shop?"

Had she? All the time. It was one of her daydreams as a little girl, one that returned periodically in adulthood. Now, though, she simply shook her head. Really, what was the point in saying or doing otherwise? It had been nothing more than a dream—one that belonged to a different time in her life.

"You should. That kind of thing would be a hit around here."

She balanced her chin on her knuckles. "I remember this little craft shop in Missouri. I stumbled across it during an outing into the country. The owner had such a variety of things for sale and people were buying them left and right."

"And how would you stack up?"

"Pretty well except for the fact I don't know how to knit." Maggie stared off into the distance, surprised how clearly she recalled everything about that craft shop. "I've wanted to learn ever since."

The thump of Rory's hand on the table pulled her back to the present. "Well, see? There you go. You've got yourself a wish."

"A wish?"

"That's right. Wanting to do something can most definitely qualify as a wish."

He popped the last bite of waffle into his mouth as she took in his strong jawline, the spots in his cheeks where dimples formed when he smiled and the faint lines that graced the outer corners of his eyes. There was something about Rory O'Brien that made her relax. Something that made her think she could actually do more than just exist through the day, as she had since Jack and Natalie…

Jack and Natalie.

Reality hit like a splash of ice water and she sat up in panic. Somehow, some way, time had passed without so much as a thought or a memory…

"Maggie? You okay?"

She yanked open her purse, fished around inside until she found a twenty-dollar bill and thrust it in his direction, his look of surprise barely registering. "I have to go back. *Now.*"

"Now? Why?"

"Because I'm fooling myself with this whole baby-step nonsense. It's either got to be one or the other," she said as tears welled in her eyes.

"One or the other? I don't understand."

"It's been an hour, Rory. A whole *hour.*"

"Oh, I'm sorry. I didn't know you had somewhere to be." He waved aside the money as he scooted out from the booth. "Did you forget an appointment?"

"No. I forgot *them.*"

Chapter Four

It took every ounce of willpower not to bust her door down and pull her into his arms, her gut-wrenching sobs on the other side twisting his stomach into knots. But she'd been adamant he leave.

Her pleas to be alone were still running in a continuous loop in his mind, warring with the urge to play knight in shining armor. For the life of him Rory couldn't understand what he'd done to change her beautiful, albeit tentative, smile into a look of complete and utter sadness the likes of which he never wanted to see on her face again.

He racked his brain for anything that could offer an explanation for the sudden shift in Maggie's mood, but he came up empty. One minute she'd been wistfully happy and the next...

"I forgot them."

Leaning his head against the oak panel, he closed his eyes against an image of the woman whose sobs seeped through the gap beneath the door. All he'd wanted to do when he invited her to breakfast was give her a distraction and him some extra time with the woman whose face had drifted in and out of his dreams all night long. Yet somehow he'd made things worse for her.

"I forgot them."

He sucked in a breath as her words came back to him yet again, the pain with which they were spoken mirrored by the agony in her eyes. Maggie was in a bad place and it was killing him not to be able to help.

Unable to handle her sobs any longer, he wandered down the hallway and into the room where they'd sat together just two hours earlier. How could they have gone from something resembling banter to this?

The key to that was in the silver cradle and the scar on Maggie's arm. That much he knew. It was just the what, how and why that had him in the dark—crucial pieces in the puzzle that was Maggie Monroe.

He grabbed his tool belt from the lumber pile where he'd left it, and secured it around his waist. As he lifted the hammer from its holder, he glanced down at the package that was responsible for placing the woman down the hall in the center of his thoughts.

He sat down beside the box and removed its lid. Light reflected off the silver ball, making it shimmer against the pillow of red velvet that lined the box.

A soft whistle escaped his lips.

Doug Rigsby sure knew how to pick a beautiful gift. But as pretty as the ornament was, the notion behind it made it even more special.

"Wishes," Rory whispered. "Who doesn't like to make wishes?"

The question was barely out before he found an answer.

Maggie.

But why? Wishes were like dreams. They gave a person hope—something to reach toward. She knew the importance of hope. It had turned her life around once already. So why couldn't she see its power now?

When he'd been no more than six years old he'd wished for his own tool set. When he'd been a teenager he'd wished for a truck while all his male classmates dreamed of Mustangs. And even when he'd been stuck behind a desk in corporate hell, the notion of one day being able to do what he truly wanted had kept him going.

Wishes made life's steps lighter. So why did Maggie dislike the notion of making a wish? Especially when she obviously had some.

Such as learning to knit.

"Learning to knit," he said aloud. "She wants to learn to knit."

Maybe it wasn't the wish itself that Maggie shied away from so much as the fear of it not coming true.

Feeling the corners of his mouth beginning to inch upward, he pulled his cell phone from the back pocket of his jeans and scrolled through his saved numbers, stopping on a familiar name.

ONE BY ONE SHE PLACED each tissue-wrapped ornament into the box, her tear-induced hiccups nearly drowning out the slight rustle they made as the stack grew higher and higher. She'd tried, she really had. But it was simply too hard.

She wanted to move forward, wanted to make her

family proud, but not this way. Not by layering new memories over the top of treasured ones.

Besides, Christmas was about family. And without Jack and Natalie, she had no family.

Wiping her hand over her burning eyes, she surveyed the room one last time. She had them all—the first Christmas ornament she'd shared with Jack after their wedding, the Snoopy computer ornament she'd given him after he landed his dream job, the miniature craft-basket ornament he'd given her on their second Christmas together and the assortment of homemade ones they'd brought from their respective childhoods.

It was hard to believe it was only a year ago they'd last hung them. Especially when she had trouble remembering certain particulars, such as which carols had been playing in the background, and the kind of flavored hot chocolate Jack had liked best.

"Peppermint," she whispered with a slight smile. Suddenly, the previous year slipped away and images flooded her mind of the day they'd tugged their tree through the door and set about the task of decorating it for the family of three they'd become.

More determined than ever to keep from clouding her past with the present, Maggie grabbed hold of the tape gun beside her foot and ran it across the top of the box. It didn't matter that the tree her uncle had left for her was bare. She was the only one there, wasn't she? And besides, the solitary star she'd managed to secure to the top was kind of pretty all on its own.

Like a wishing star shining in the night sky.

A *wishing* star.

Scooting the box to the side, she rocked back on her heels and looked up at the delicate star on the very top of the tree. For as long as she could remember she'd loved making wishes. On birthday candles, on pennies thrown into fountains, on shooting stars...

Those wishes had brought her Jack. And when the time was right, Natalie.

Now, Maggie had no more wishes left. Unless wishing for another day with them could truly happen.

But what if Rory was right? What if wishes could also apply to smaller things? Things a person wanted to do or accomplish? And if he *was* right, perhaps her desire to make her family proud could be a wish—one she'd realized, at least on a small scale, just a few hours earlier when she'd eaten her first real meal in more months than she could count.

Breakfast isn't enough, Maggie.

Shaking her head at the voice in her head, she blinked against the brightness of the star. "It's a step, Jack. And for now it has to be enough."

A strange sound made her turn just in time to see a mint-green envelope appear beneath the door and slide across the hardwood in her direction.

"What on earth?" she mumbled as she grabbed hold of it. The sight of her name written in a masculine scrawl made her breath hitch. Turning the envelope over, she allowed her fingers to linger on the sealed flap for just a moment before giving in to curiosity.

Carefully, she slid the matching green paper from the envelope and unfolded it, to find a nine-word sentence that caught her by surprise.

Redeemable for one FREE knitting lesson in your home.

She rubbed her right and then her left eye before reading the words once again.

Redeemable for one FREE knitting lesson in your home.

"A knitting lesson?" she whispered. "What on—"

A soft knock made her look up, the green stationery clutched in her hand. "Yes?" she called in confusion.

"Maggie? It's Delilah."

Delilah?

"I met you, or rather, met you again, earlier this morning. I was the crazy woman who badgered your eating companion."

Maggie rose to her feet and approached the door, a multitude of questions swirling in her thoughts. Yanking it open, she came face-to-face with the woman from the diner. "Wow. H-hi. Wow. This is certainly a surprise."

Delilah's graying head bobbed ever so slightly as a smile revealed the faintest hint of a dimple in her left cheek. "I imagine it is. But I've never been known for my predictability. Except with my cooking, of course."

There was something about this woman that called to Maggie, something so open, so real it was hard to ignore. Maybe it was the happiness she exuded via the laugh lines that framed her friendly eyes. Maybe it was the way she'd stopped at every booth that morning, treating each and every customer as if they were part of her family. Maybe it was the way she had noted Maggie's lack of weight, yet hadn't hounded her with unwanted advice and disapproving comments.

"Breakfast. This morning. It was delicious. It helped me—" Maggie shifted from foot to foot as she searched for just the right words "—take a step I needed to take."

If her words were cryptic, the woman didn't let on. "I'm glad. And I hope you'll come back again. And bring that big galoot with you."

"Big galoot?"

"Rory." Maggie couldn't help but laugh as the woman continued. "From the time he first marched into my diner with a plastic hammer in one hand and a block of wood in the other, he had me captivated. Why, that young man had the most flawless manners of any child I'd ever seen, and boy, could he talk your ear off. There he'd be, pouring syrup over his pancakes and chatting up a storm while Reardon simply sat there, listening. Two peas in a pod they were. Though how they came from the same pod was always a mystery. Woo-wee, those boys were different. Different as night and day. While Rory was always making things with his hands, Reardon was lost in the pages of a book. While Rory had an appetite that never quit, Reardon would push his food around his plate, hoping no one would notice he hadn't eaten. But I noticed. I always noticed those boys. Except when it…" Delilah suddenly went quiet. "Would you listen to me go? Seems I've got a little chatterbox in me, too."

"It helps drown out the silence."

Delilah cocked her head and studied Maggie as understanding dawned in her pale green eyes. "The silence is painful at times, isn't it?"

Maggie swallowed with difficulty. "It can be," she whispered.

"Then how about we set that off to the side for a little bit and try something new."

She felt her brows furrow. "Something new? I don't understand."

Lifting a basket into the air, Delilah jutted her chin in the direction of Maggie's left hand. "I'm here so you can redeem *that*."

"I don't—" She stopped, looked down at the paper still clutched in her hand. "You mean this is from you?"

The woman shook her head.

"Then how did you know—wait!" Maggie felt a flutter in her chest as the pieces fell into place. "Rory sent you, didn't he?"

"He said you've always wanted to learn to knit. And since I love to knit almost as much as I love to cook, he thought I could help you with—"

"With my *wish*," she finished, her words barely audible amid the sudden acceleration of her heart.

Realizing Delilah's gaze was still locked on her face, Maggie forced her mind away from the swirling emotions in the pit of her stomach and back to the woman in front of her. "You don't have to do this. Really. I know you must be busy at the diner."

"That's what employees are for, dear. And besides, how often does a person get to play fairy godmother in their lifetime?"

Fairy godmother...

"Though, technically, I think that title belongs more to Rory than it does me."

Rory…

"So, would you like to bring some chairs out into the hallway or would you prefer to work inside?"

The woman's words finally registered, as did Maggie's lack of hostess skills. "Oh. Oh, I'm sorry. Please…please come in." Stepping to the side to allow the woman entry into her suite, she rushed to offer an explanation for their less than tidy surroundings. "You'll have to excuse the boxes. I was just—"

"Decorating?" The woman stopped in the center of the living room and smiled up at the bare branches of the tree. "I finished mine just last night. And I did a good job, if I do say so myself. Though if I don't quit buying new ornaments every year, I may need a third tree."

"A third tree?" Maggie echoed.

"A third tree. I love decorating. I love the way it transforms the house into this magical place where hope is as ever-present as the pine needles I'll be sweeping up on a daily basis over the next four or five weeks."

"Hope?"

Delilah nodded. "For something better. Richer."

Maggie felt her shoulders slump. Maybe that's why she couldn't decorate. Because she'd already *had* better. In fact, she'd had the best.

Forcing her thoughts from the realization that threatened to zap her energy, she motioned toward the sofa. "Can I get you an apple? Or a glass of water?"

"That would be wonderful, but only if you join me."

"Oh, I'm fine. I had a really big breakfast."

Delilah tsked softly under her breath. "That was hours

ago, dear. Besides, once we start knitting you'll lose all track of time. Trust me on this."

Maggie considered protesting, but opted instead to retrieve two apples and two glasses of water from the kitchen before claiming a spot on the sofa beside the woman. "It was really nice of you to come here."

"I'd do anything for Rory. Especially something that means as much to him as this apparently does."

She felt her face flush. "I didn't ask him to do this."

The woman set the basket between them and began pulling items from it onto her lap. "I know. In fact, Rory made that perfectly clear when we talked earlier. But he wanted to do this. For you."

"But I—"

Delilah's plump hand closed over hers and squeezed. "You want to learn to knit, yes?"

Maggie nodded.

"Then let's learn, shall we?"

Blinking against the familiar tears that were there for unfamiliar reasons, she nodded once again.

And so she learned. About yarn, and knitting needles, and the proper way to hold her hands…

Little by little she surrendered to the process—to the feel of the yarn at her fingertips, to the thrill of learning something new, to the excitement that came with watching each step turn into something real.

"Is this what I'd do to make a scarf?" she asked as she looked up from the rectangle taking shape in her lap.

"Yes, it is." Delilah reached into the basket, extracted a few more skeins of yarn and set them on the coffee table in front of the sofa. "I brought along some extra yarn so you could try whenever you want."

Maggie set down her knitting. "I can't take that. You've already done so much."

Delilah's hand closed over hers once again. "It's part of the lesson."

"Part of the lesson?"

The woman nodded, her eyes shining. "Rory wanted me to teach you. And he wanted you to be able to start creating whatever it is you always imagined knitting." Releasing Maggie's hand, Delilah reached into the basket once again. "See this book? It's one of the best step-by-step guides out there. But if you have a problem or don't understand something, call me. Or better yet, stop by the diner. Maybe we can work you up to a whole order of waffles."

Maggie couldn't help but laugh. "Even if I had been eating over the past ten months I'm not sure I could ever consume that much."

Delilah's eyes led Maggie's to the silver framed photograph she'd set on the corner table just that morning. "Is that when you lost them? Ten months ago?"

"Ten months and twenty-three days ago," she said, her voice cracking. "And I'm not sure the pain will ever stop."

For a moment, the woman said nothing, Maggie's words hovering above them like a wet blanket that threatened to smother the companionable atmosphere. But finally Delilah spoke, her words catching Maggie by surprise.

"And I suspect it won't. But in time you'll find a place to put that pain, so you can let the joy take over."

"Joy?" She shook her head. "There isn't any joy."

"You looked happy when you were at the diner this morning. You and Rory talked over your food like you were old friends."

She closed her eyes against the memory, the reminder of her betrayal akin to a slap across the face. "And it was wrong."

Delilah gasped. "What was wrong?"

"All of it. The laughing. The dreaming. The forgetting."

"Laughing isn't wrong if it's done out of happiness. Dreaming is essential because it gives us wings, and forgetting…well, there's a difference between living and forgetting."

Drawing a skein of yarn to her chest, Maggie met Delilah's eyes. "Living?"

"That's what you do with life, isn't it?"

Her throat tightened. "But I—"

Not unkindly, Delilah removed the yarn from Maggie's hands and set it gently in her lap. "Ten months and twenty-three days ago wasn't your time. It was—" the woman's eyes returned to the photograph ever so briefly "—theirs. Remember that."

Chapter Five

No matter what his head knew to be true, his heart still had a hard time accepting the fact that Reardon was gone. Part of that, Rory knew, was the suddenness. When a person was sick for a long period of time it gave family members a chance to prepare and imagine. To brace for the inevitable.

Suicide didn't. Instead, it came without warning, leaving an unending supply of what-ifs and if-onlys in its wake.

Rory soaked up every detail of the face in the photograph—the dark brown hair, the sky-blue eyes, the angular jawline. They'd been identical twins, their outward features mirror images of one another. Yet when it came to the stuff inside—the stuff that made them tick—they'd been so different.

But still, he should have known. Twins were supposed to have a sixth sense when it came to one another, weren't they?

Shaking his head against the ever-present pang of regret, he returned the frame to its rightful spot on the mantel, a familiar voice replaying in his thoughts for the umpteenth time in the past hour.

"You can't fix everything in life, Rory. Some things need time and space."

He'd waited all evening for Delilah's call, hoping she'd have some insight into Maggie's hurt. Insight that could help him understand the woman who'd captured his attention in a matter of moments and held on to it ever since. And she had, her explanation for Maggie's pain bringing everything into focus.

A car accident had claimed the lives of Maggie's husband and baby daughter. They'd died on impact, leaving Maggie injured and alone.

It was a loss he couldn't even imagine. Not completely, anyway. But he certainly understood the sadness, knew how it chipped away at everything in its path, including hope.

And when a person lost hope…

He glanced back at his brother's face, raking a hand through his hair as he did so. People like Delilah meant well. He knew that. He believed that. But he also knew they didn't understand.

How could they?

But *he* did. Leaving someone alone with their grief was a bad move. It took options away—options he refused to miss out on this time around.

SHE LEANED TOWARD THE mirror and studied her efforts closely. Sure enough, the black circles that shadowed her eyes were virtually gone, their presence masked by the foundation she'd unearthed at the bottom of her purse.

"That's what you get for staying up all night," Maggie muttered as she pulled back, sticking her tongue out at her reflection in the process.

And it was true. Only this time she hadn't stayed up because of nightmares or the kind of memories that left her in a cold sweat. No, this time she'd spent the night sitting on her sofa.

Knitting.

For hours after Delilah had left, Maggie had flipped through the guidebook, trying various stitches again and again until she felt she was ready to tackle an actual project. Then, armed with a navy blue yarn, she'd knitted from dusk until dawn, her very first attempt at a scarf earning an N for Not Too Bad.

Tugging her pale blue sweater down around her hips, she took one final look in the mirror. She owed Rory another apology—this time for being such a downer the previous day. And when she was done, she'd thank him. For granting a wish she hadn't realized meant so much.

She inhaled every ounce of determination she could muster into her lungs, then opened the door to the hall-way, turning back just as quickly.

Should she bring it?

Shaking off the momentary hesitation that threatened to curtail yet another step forward, she strode over to the sofa and reached for the scarf. When people brought a plate of cookies to a neighbor, it was polite to return said plate with a different treat, right? So wouldn't the same hold true for someone who gave you a knitting lesson? Maggie wasn't entirely sure, but tucked the scarf under her arm anyway as she headed toward the distant sound of a hammer.

When she reached the same room she'd visited just twenty-four hours earlier, she stopped, gazing at the frame Rory had erected around the fireplace on the far wall. "Are those going to be built-in benches?" she asked from the doorway.

The hammering stopped.

"Maggie? Is that you?"

"One and the same," she said, before nibbling her lower lip.

He peeked around a corner, surprise chased from his eyes by the smile that lit his face and brought a tingle down her spine. "Well, aren't you a sight for sore eyes?"

"I—I…" She stopped, unsure of what to say next.

For a moment he simply looked at her. Then he pointed toward the fireplace. "You asked about that frame?"

She nodded.

"Well, you're absolutely right. There's going to be a built-in bench on either side of the fireplace. I imagine your uncle is going to put some sort of—"

"Cushions on them. Cushions with a bold stripe, accompanied by a few throw pillows reflecting the colors of the stripes—warm hues that'll make you want to curl up beside a roaring fire and read. Or think." She inhaled the image into her mind, and smiled. "Can't you just picture it?"

He slipped his hammer into his tool belt and nodded. "I can now. Wow. You really painted a picture in my mind with that description."

A flash of warmth flooded her cheeks. "It was easy because it came straight from my memory. That's the way this suite looked when I was a kid. It was the one my uncle used to live in before he took over the one he's in now. I spent a lot of hours on those benches, dreaming."

"What kind of dreaming?"

"About having my own family again one day," she said. The sadness from earlier threatened to send her scurrying back to her room, but she waved the memory away. "Sorry about that."

"Don't apologize." He gestured toward the frame. "As a carpenter, I see the structure. You, as a crafter, see ways to make it inviting. It's the difference between plainness and style."

"You think what you do is plain?" she asked.

He shrugged. "I love what I create, I really do. I have no desire to do anything else. But when I'm done with my part, it's just a room. When someone like you is done, it's a home."

She studied him for a moment, noting the intensity in his eyes as he studied his work. "I think you're short-changing yourself. Your work is…" she looked around at the built-in benches, the molding around the bay window, the beams that graced the ceiling above her head "…beautiful. I can see why my uncle hired you to restore this old place."

Had she blinked, she would have missed the surprise that flashed across his face. "Surely you know that, right?"

His face reddened ever so slightly. "If I did, it was my

own ego putting it there. Hearing it from you is a million times more special."

"Then I'm glad I said it. Because it's true." She looked down at her hands and remembered her reasons for being there. "Look, I wanted to apologize. For breakfast yesterday."

He took a step in her direction. "Don't. It was the best breakfast I've had in…well, *ever,* if I'm honest with myself."

She felt her cheeks flush warmer still as she met his eyes and saw the raw honesty in them. "I mean about the way breakfast ended. It's just that I feel so guilty when time slips by and I realize I haven't thought about…" She felt a familiar sting in her eyes.

He stepped closer. "Just because you're not aware of a thought doesn't mean it's not in your heart."

Her head snapped up. "You really believe that?"

For a moment he didn't answer, the only indication he'd heard her being the way he tilted his head. "Will you come sit with me for a moment?" He gestured toward the lumber pile that had served as their couch just twenty-four hours earlier.

She considered objecting, but in the end simply stepped inside the room and sat down, the tingle from earlier resurfacing as he took his place beside her.

He let go of a long deep breath before turning to face her. "Eighteen months ago I lost my twin brother, Reardon. It was fast and it was unexpected."

"Did he die in an accident, too?" she asked as she searched for, and found, the all-too-familiar pain in Rory's eyes.

"Yes. But of his own doing."

She sucked in her breath, regretting the sound almost instantly. "I'm so sorry."

"So am I." Rory clasped his hands behind his head, only to drop them to his lap once again. "I knew he was struggling after he broke up with his fiancée. I saw it. With my own two eyes. But I figured he just needed a little time."

Without thinking, Maggie covered Rory's hand with her own and gave it a gentle squeeze. "That certainly seems reasonable."

He shrugged. "But it was wrong. What he needed was someone to hold him up."

"You couldn't have known that."

"I *should* have. He was my brother. My twin brother." With a flip of his hand, he entwined his fingers with hers. "After he did it, I thought about him constantly. Heard his laugh, imagined his face, smelled that damn cologne he always wore, you name it. That's lessened a little in the past few months, but it doesn't mean he's not in my heart. He'll always be there."

She closed her eyes as Rory's words washed over her. On some level she knew he was right—knew that just because she'd enjoyed his company over breakfast didn't mean she'd forgotten her family. But still…

"Heck, he's everywhere. My heart, my head, my everything."

"Your everything?" she asked.

"Yeah. Without even realizing it, I let him guide me into this field." He waved his free hand around the room. "Not that this hasn't always been my passion, because it has. But until Reardon's death, I simply saw carpentry as this pie in the sky."

"His death changed that?"

"In many ways, yes. It showed me how fleeting and unpredictable life can be."

She pondered Rory's words. "And so that was the push you needed to pursue your passion?"

He shrugged again. "Maybe there was a tiny bit of that in my decision to get out from behind a desk, but I also think it was the desire to do what I failed to do with him."

"What do you mean?" she asked, willing herself to focus on the conversation rather than the feel of his hand in hers.

"I should have found a way to fix him. Instead, I stood by and figured he'd get it together on his own."

Maggie looked up at Rory as his voice faltered. She knew about second-guessing. She did it all the time. What if she and Jack had heeded the weather reports and stayed home that night? What if they hadn't missed their turn? What if she hadn't forgotten Natalie's diaper bag, and they had been able to keep going?

There was so much she wished she could say to wipe the regret off Rory's face. But it was hard to sell something she had trouble buying, too.

The tightening of his hand around hers broke through her thoughts. "Hey, I didn't mean to pull you down with my inability to fix things."

Fix things…

With a gentle tug, she freed herself from his grasp and

grabbed hold of her creation. "You fixed something of mine."

His eyebrows furrowed. "Oh yeah? What's that?"

"You took away my last mental excuse for not opening a gift shop one day."

"I took away... Ohh. You mean the coupon?"

"Yes. The coupon. Delilah stopped by yesterday afternoon and taught me how to knit."

He grinned. "And? How'd you do?"

"Why don't you tell me?" Maggie held out the scarf. "But remember...fine detail isn't your thing, okay?"

He looked at her, clearly puzzled.

"Which means you won't notice the mistakes—deal?"

His laugh echoed around the room. "Deal." Taking the scarf from her hands, he unfolded it and looked it over from top to bottom. "Delilah helped you with this?"

"She showed me how to knit. I made the scarf after she left."

"You made this after she left? Wait. She was just there yesterday. How long did this take you?"

"I finished about an hour ago." Leaning to the right, Maggie studied her handiwork once again.

"You worked on this all night?"

She nodded. "It helped me bypass a few nightmares."

"I guess I should lecture you on the importance of sleep at this moment but—" he held up the scarf "—this is too good."

"You really think so?" The breathless tone in her voice made her cringe inwardly.

"I really *know* so."

"Then I know it's going to an appreciative home," she quipped.

He stared at her. "You made this for me?"

Fiddling with a corner of the scarf that draped across her leg, she nodded. "It's the least I could do after you set up that lesson and all."

"You had a wish. And I had an in for making it happen."

"A wish," she repeated.

"A *little* wish," he corrected. Lifting the scarf once again, he looped it around his neck and leaped to his feet. With six quick strides he was across the room and back again, a familiar gift box in his hands. "You left this here yesterday."

"I know."

He handed it to her. She handed it back.

"Don't you want to hang it on your tree?"

"I've decided not to decorate a tree this year, after all."

"C'mon, you have—"

She cut him off midprotest. "I just can't. But it would mean a lot to me if you hung it on your tree instead."

He looked from her to the ornament and back again. "My tree?"

"Yes, your tree. Besides, you're better at this wishing stuff than I am."

"I don't know, Maggie. That's not what your uncle wanted."

"Please?"

For a moment he said nothing, then he met her gaze

with a mischievous one of his own. "Okay, okay. But under two conditions."

"And those are?" she prodded, a smile twitching her own lips.

"First, you tell me another one of your wishes. A small one."

She considered his words, an answer forming instantly. "To never forget. Ever."

He nodded, his eyes never leaving hers.

"And you?" she asked, fighting to keep the moment light.

"To fix things."

"Well—" she glanced around the room "—it certainly looks like you're off to a good start."

"Maybe. But I have other things to fix, too." He lifted the ornament box into her line of vision. "Which kind of leads me to my second condition."

Rolling her eyes skyward, she made a silly face, the sound of Rory's subsequent laugh chasing away the perpetual chill in her body. "And that is?"

"That you'll let me fix you dinner tonight. At my place."

Chapter Six

Whether it was the all-night knitting session or the visit with Rory, Maggie wasn't sure. But one thing was certain—she hadn't slept so hard or so well in months.

Ten months and twenty-four days, to be exact.

And if it wasn't for the chirp of her phone reminding her to get up, she'd still be sleeping. Soundly.

If she'd had any dreams, she didn't remember them. If she'd had any nightmares, they hadn't been bad enough to wake her. All she knew was the time on the clock when she'd climbed into bed and the time there now: 6:15.

Glancing down at the directions Rory had written out, she couldn't help but smile. For the first time in as many days as she hadn't slept, she actually found herself looking forward to the evening.

It didn't matter what he cooked or if he could even cook at all. The simple notion of having a little company actually sounded okay. Good, even.

And it made sense. Rory O'Brien was a nice man. He was sweet and funny and intelligent and…

Indisputably handsome.

She shook her head and examined the map he'd drawn

for her that morning, the path to his home clearly marked out. They would have dinner, he'd said. Then, if they were both game, they could pop in a movie or simply talk.

It had sounded good, fun even—an invitation she'd tried, but failed, to duck. And she was glad.

Why the change of heart, she wasn't sure. Perhaps it was the seven-hour nap she'd just taken. Perhaps it was the unexpected burst of energy and positive thinking the knitting lesson had created. Or perhaps it was the simple fact that Rory *understood*.

Setting the directions on the table beside the door, she turned slowly in front of the mirror. The brushed jeans fit her okay, though a few extra pounds would make them look better.

She lifted her hand to her neck, fingered the tiny diamond pendant that hung from the gold chain nestled in the V of her cashmere sweater. The necklace had been a gift from Jack just six months after they'd started dating. During their subsequent years together he'd given her other necklaces, more expensive ones to reflect his budding career, but it was this one she wore most often.

Feeling her excitement begin to wane at the memory, she grabbed the directions and her keys and stepped into the hall.

HE HEARD HER FOOTSTEPS before the knock, and felt the relief they unleashed in his body. He'd been so certain she would change her mind once she got back to her suite. That she'd think better of accepting his invitation.

But she hadn't and he was glad. Real glad.

Yanking the door open, he felt his breath hitch at the sight of her standing on his front step—her long brown hair cascading over her shoulders in soft waves, the sensual curve of her lips, her dark brown eyes glistening in the glow of the porch light as they looked shyly back at him….

Oh man, he was in trouble.

"Maggie…you made it." He stepped to the side and motioned her in. "Any problem with the directions?"

"No. They were great but—" Two steps into the hall, she stopped and peered up at him with a look he'd bet good money didn't bode well for their evening. "I wanted to bring something—a pie or a cake. But the bakery closed at five. I'm sorry."

He felt the sudden tension in his shoulders ease. "That's okay. It would have only delayed your arrival, and I already made dessert."

Following her gaze down to her gloved hands, he knew he wasn't out of the woods yet. Being here was tough on her. He could see it in the way she slid the tiny diamond pendant back and forth along the gold chain she wore, could sense it in the way she looked at her feet again and again.

"That's a beautiful necklace, Maggie."

Startled, she looked up, a flash of pain crackling across her face.

Uh-oh.

"Can I take your coat?" he asked quickly as he met her wary eyes with what he hoped was an encouraging smile. "I made a fire and things are getting mighty toasty around here."

"I'm not sure if I should really—"

"Ohhh, I almost forgot. C'mon with me for a second. I want you to see how it looks on my tree." Tucking her arm in his, he set off in the direction of the hearth room. If he didn't act fast, she was going to leave. That much he could figure out.

He also knew he didn't want her to leave. Not yet, anyway. Not until they had a chance to spend some more time together. The key, though, was finding something that would make her relax, make her *want* to stay.

"How what looks?" she asked, her words morphing into a whisper as he pulled her through the archway and stopped in front of the tree. "Oh, Rory, it's lovely—the tree, the ornaments, all of it."

He beamed. "I think so, too."

And suddenly the ice was broken. Whatever reluctance or hesitation or second-guessing he'd sensed upon her arrival was gone.

Slowly, she made her way around the tree, reaching out from time to time to examine a particular ornament, each move she made captivating him more.

Maggie looked different somehow. Her face seemed softer, more relaxed. And her eyes—those large brown, doelike eyes that had drifted in and out of his thoughts all day—actually held a hint of a sparkle.

"What's this one?" she asked, brushing a gentle finger across a homemade snowflake that resembled a star. "Did you make it?"

"I sure did. In Mrs. Trantini's kindergarten classroom. It was a present for my mom."

Maggie looked from the ornament to him, his body tightening in response. "Why do you have it then?"

Keeping his eyes locked on hers, he shrugged. "It was one of the ones I claimed after she passed away."

Maggie looked back at the tree. "Doesn't that make it hard? Seeing it hanging on your tree…reminding you of a time that's forever gone?"

"But it's not gone," he insisted. "Seeing it there, hanging on my tree, helps me remember. And I do. I remember how long it took to cut all the holes just right. I remember how I searched all over the house for the perfect gift box so it wouldn't accidentally rip when my mom unwrapped it on Christmas morning. I remember the way her eyes glistened when she opened it. And I remember how she insisted on hanging it at the front of the tree each year from then on…like it was some sort of priceless keepsake."

"But hanging it now on your own tree, when you're by yourself… That doesn't cloud out the memories?"

"Nope. It just helps me remember even more."

Maggie released the snowflake and backed away from the tree. "I see."

"Can I take your coat now? Dinner should be ready shortly."

In a flash he saw her shoulders stiffen as the internal war from earlier intensified. Only this time he suspected any gray areas had dissipated in favor of two distinct sides. Should she stay? Should she go? He prayed she'd opt for the former.

Her eyes closed for just a moment, only to reopen with

what sounded like a sigh of determination. "It smells good. Have you been cooking long?"

He sent up a mental prayer of thanks as he watched her wiggle out of her coat. "A couple of years, I guess. I got tired of eating standard bachelor fare."

"TV dinners and soup?" she teased, the sudden lilt to her voice bringing a smile to his lips.

"On good days, yeah." He draped her coat over the back of a corner chair, then turned to face her once again, the sight of her long legs and feminine features doing their best to distract him from the subject at hand. "You... you look great, Maggie."

She glanced down at her body, the surprise on her face captivating him all the more. "You really think so?"

"How could I not?" he asked honestly.

"Well, for starters, I'm too thin. A by-product of not eating, no doubt."

"Which you took steps to change yesterday at breakfast."

Nodding, she continued. "And my inability to sleep has earned circles under my eyes the likes of which most raccoons would be embarrassed by."

The circles. That was what was different. "I don't see any circles."

A small laugh escaped her lips. "Makeup can hide almost anything. The fact that I just slept for seven hours certainly helped, too."

"All I know is that you're beautiful. I'd be blind not to see that." And he meant it.

Crimson rose in her cheeks, prompting him to redirect the conversation into safer waters. "Do you like lasagna?"

Her face lit up. "I love it!"

"Then we're in luck." Slipping a hand against the small of her back, he guided her toward the kitchen, the crackling of the fire in the hearth doing little to drown out the pounding in his chest. "I set the table just before you got here, but wasn't sure what you'd like to drink. I've got red wine, diet soda and bottled water."

"Water would be fine, thank you."

He followed her gaze around the table, watched as it lingered on the place settings for two before moving on to the candle he'd lit in the middle. Worried he'd overdone things, he searched for something to say to lighten the moment. Something that would undo the sudden tension he felt. "The first cake I made this evening actually burned. I lit that candle in the hopes it would mask any lingering smell from my faux pas."

Her body sagged ever so slightly as she tilted her nose up and sniffed. "It certainly seems to be working."

"I'm glad." He pointed to a chair. "Why don't you take a seat? Everything should be ready. I just need to grab the salad from the refrigerator and the lasagna from the oven."

And so it went—dinner, drinks, conversation, laughter, and occasional awkward moments that had nearly disappeared by the time they were done.

"Why don't we bring our drinks into the hearth room," he suggested, the hopeful note in his voice one he simply couldn't hide. He enjoyed Maggie's company, plain and simple. She was sweet, honest, serious, funny and utterly endearing—all things that guaranteed she'd remain in his thoughts, as she had since they'd met. Only now they'd be mixed with a longing he could no longer rationalize away. Not if the way his body reacted to her was any indication. Especially when he felt her skin beneath his palm, as he did while guiding her to the sofa.

What was it about her that made him feel like an awkward teenager? It wasn't as if he hadn't been in the company of women in some crazy length of time. Because he had. And he'd been confident with every single one of them.

Yet somehow Maggie was different. Sure, he imagined what it would be like to pull her close, to feel her body against his. He'd be a fool if he didn't. But there was more, too.

Like a desire to see her smile. And a need to keep her safe.

He pointed toward the tree, his body keenly aware of her proximity on the sofa. "I filled out one of the slips."

She stilled her glass midway to her lips. "What slips?"

"You know, for the wishing ball. The little slips of paper that you're supposed to write your wishes on. I even put it inside."

"Do you think it'll come true?" she whispered as she set her water on the coffee table.

"I guess we'll find out next year when I open it again." He studied her for a moment, enchanted by the way the colorful lights of the tree reflected in Maggie's eyes. "Would you like to write one?"

She held up her palms. "No. I don't really have any wishes left."

"That's not true."

He reached for her hand as she turned to him with a frown. "Excuse me?"

"Well, there was the one about knitting, right?"

"Which you granted, remember?"

Nodding, he continued. "And then there was the one from earlier today."

"I don't remember making a wish."

"You did. In fact, we both did."

A smile played across her kissable mouth and he felt his chest tighten in response. "That's right. You wished to fix things. Like tonight's dinner."

"How'd I do?"

"Amazing. It was absolutely delicious."

He puffed out his chest with a playful air. "Just call me Chef Extraordinaire."

"But that was *your* wish, Mr. Chef. I don't remember having one for me."

"I do." Reluctantly, he released her hand long enough to open the drawer of the coffee table and extract a gift-wrapped box. "Which is why you should open this," he said as he placed the square object in her lap.

"What did you do?" she whispered.

"Just open it."

For a moment, as she stared down at the gift, he thought she was going to decline. But eventually she turned it over, her fingers finding the taped seams.

He heard her startled gasp as the paper fell to the side. "What's this?"

Scooting closer on the sofa, he ran his hand along the cover of the leather-bound book he'd purchased after work. "It's a journaling album—a place to keep your memories close and your fear of forgetting at bay."

Chapter Seven

She stared at the book in her lap, the fine golden trim sparkling in the glow from the firelight. For more moments than were polite she said nothing, the thudding of her heart drowning out all thoughts except one.

Glancing up, she met Rory's eyes, her trembling mouth making it difficult to form the words she wanted to speak.

Slowly, his finger touched her lips. "You don't have to say a word, Maggie. The look in your eyes says it all." He let his hand fall to his lap, his gaze never leaving hers. "And you are so very, very welcome. I hope you like it."

"*Like* it?" she whispered as she looked from him to the book and back again. "Like it? I—I *love* it."

The smile that swept across his face was impossible to miss. So, too, was the naked relief there. "How did you know?" she asked.

"It was the wish you shared this morning—about not wanting to forget." He slung his arm over the back of the sofa, its proximity to her neck making her swallow. Hard.

She searched for something to say to distract herself from the sensations running along the tops of her shoulders. She was so very aware of Rory's nearness. And warmth. And confidence. And sweetness…

"I guess I'm hoping that by writing down some of your special memories, you'll have an additional way to visit them when you need to."

"Additional?"

"The first place they are is in your heart and your mind. Writing them in this book just gives you one more place to go and remember." He nodded while opening the book to the first page. "But what's neat about this journal is that there's a spot on each page where you can add a picture or a ticket stub or some other tangible item that goes along with your memory."

She leaned her head back against the sofa, his strong arm offering a sense of safety she hadn't realized she needed until she felt it. "I remember the day I found out I was pregnant. I actually took a picture of the pink line."

"The pink line?"

Turning her head, she gazed up at him. "I took one of those home pregnancy tests. No line, not pregnant. Pink line, pregnant."

"Ahh. See, I've never had a child, so this is new to me." He scooted a hairbreadth closer. "But that sure sounds like a great picture to include on the page where you recall that moment in your life."

She closed her eyes, letting the past wash over her.

"Tell me more."

Her eyes flew open. "You really want to hear that kind of stuff?"

"I'd love to."

For the briefest of moments she hesitated, unsure whether his request was genuine or simply the words of a man who epitomized kindness. But in the end, she spoke.

"There was the first time I took her to the zoo. I knew it was silly to go. She was too little to have a clue about what I was showing her, but…well, I loved it. The weather was perfect—a gorgeous autumn day. And the animals were in their glory, running here and there in their habitats. I told her about every animal we saw and she cooed along as if she actually understood. Even though I know she didn't."

Maggie's breath caught when she felt his hand on the side of her face. "Okay, so maybe she didn't understand the difference between an alligator and a crocodile…or even whether you were talking about the tree in front of her or the strange colored thing on the ground," Rory replied. "But I bet she understood one thing."

"What's that?"

"That she was with the one person who made her feel loved and safe and wanted. I'd coo about that, too."

A lump formed in her throat. When Maggie said nothing, he continued, his hand dropping from her face to the book. "Do you have any keepsakes from that day? Like a ticket stub or a zoo map or something?"

She swallowed back the lump, tried to focus on something other than the void left by the movement of his hand. "I have a leaf."

"A leaf?"

"A leaf," she repeated. "It floated down from a tree near the prairie-dog exhibit. She watched it drift down until it landed on her coat. And when it did, she broke out into her very first smile."

The corners of Maggie's mouth lifted upward as she returned to that day, the thought of her baby's first smile misting her eyes.

"If her smile was anything like yours, I'd want to remember it, too."

The raspy quality of his voice made her look up, their gazes meeting in the firelight. "That first smile was like nothing I'd ever seen. It was the epitome of joy…and she spread it to me. Every single day of her much too short life."

Rory's palm returned to her face, this time lingering on her cheek. "I can't imagine a better gift."

She covered his hand with her own, blinking at the tears that burned her eyes. "There isn't."

"Then savor it, Maggie. Don't let it slip away."

Savor it….

Was Rory right? Was all her moping akin to letting Natalie's precious gift slip through her fingers?

"I know you're right, Rory. I do. I really, truly do. But there are times…times like yesterday at the diner… when I'm afraid that by moving forward I'm leaving them behind. And I can't do that. I *won't* do that."

"Then don't. Keep them here—" his hand, still holding hers, lifted upward to her temple and then dropped to the center of her chest "—and here and—" he continued down to the book in her lap "—here."

Her memory journal.

Aware of his hand in hers, she offered the words she'd been wanting to say since the beginning. Words that went far beyond a standard thank-you, just as his gift went far beyond a simple gesture.

"I don't know what it is about you that makes you so thoughtful and so giving. But it's special and it's unique and it's a blessing I didn't see coming. I slept today because I spent last night knitting. And that sleep was the best rest I've had in over ten months."

"You're losing me," he said, not unkindly.

"I'm sorry. It's just that I made an offhand comment about wanting to learn to knit, and poof! You made it happen. Then today…I share a new wish with you, and once again, poof! You find a way to make that wish come true, too. I almost don't know what to say—"

"Then don't," he mumbled as he closed the gap between them, his lips finding hers and igniting a fire in her heart every bit as bright as the one crackling in the hearth.

FOR SOMEONE WHO'D VOWED not to do anything to scare her, he was sure doing a lousy job. Then again, based on the way her lips stayed on his, maybe he wasn't scaring her, after all.

But all he really knew was how good she tasted, how sweet she felt. Moving his hand to cup the back of her head, he kissed her with greater intensity, felt the way his body responded to the parting of her lips and the mingling of their tongues.

Her arms looped around his neck as the kiss deepened,

filling his body with warmth. It was like nothing he'd ever felt before and everything he wanted to feel again.

Breathing in the scent of lilacs and soap that seemed to cling to her hair, he became aware of a new taste... salt.

And as the taste finally registered, so, too, did the fact that her hands had left his neck and were now bracing against his chest, pushing him away.

He pulled back. "Maggie, what's wrong?"

"I—I can't do this. I can't. It's—" She stopped, her words morphing into a strangled cry that tore at his very soul.

"It's okay," he whispered as he reached for her hands, only to have her pull them out of his reach. "You didn't do anything wrong."

"I did *everything* wrong."

"Tell me. Tell me what you did wrong, Maggie." He watched helplessly as the tears streamed down her face until he thought he'd explode with the urge to kiss them away.

"They've only been gone a little while. I can't be doing...this." She jumped to her feet and motioned toward the tree. "I can't be decorating trees, and celebrating holidays, and making wishes, and—" A strangled cry rose up where the rest of her sentence should have been.

But he didn't need the words to know what she'd been about to say. He could finish that sentence all on his own. "And what? Kissing me?"

She looked at the floor and nodded.

He stood in turn, reaching out for her hands only

to have her snatch them back. "Maggie, there's nothing wrong with decorating a Christmas tree or celebrating a holiday or making a wish. It's what people do. It's part of life."

Her head snapped up. "You're right. It is. For people who *have* one."

"And you have one, Maggie. And so do I. It's the difference between me and my brother, and you and your family. We're here—during the Christmas season—with an ornament designed to celebrate wishes." He stepped closer, bridging the physical gap between them. "And the kiss? That happened because I feel something for you. And if the way you kissed me back is any indication, I think you feel something for me, too."

For a long moment, she said nothing, her hooded expression holding few clues to her thoughts. When she finally spoke, however, she left little room for conjecture. "I know about life. I know that it can be wonderful and intriguing and the most amazing gift imaginable. But I also know it can be taken away without warning, shaking the ground under a person's feet for a very long time. I've lived that…*twice*. The first time, I learned how to get back on my feet, if for no other reason than to have another chance. This time, I'm trying to get back on my feet for an entirely different reason."

"And what reason is that?" he asked.

"To exist. Because I have to."

"That's it? You don't want to hope?"

She shrugged. "Why? So it can shatter my heart a third time?"

Raking his fingers through his hair, he searched for

something to say to make her realize the error in her thinking. "But, Maggie...don't you see it doesn't have to be that way?"

"For me it does."

Chapter Eight

No matter what she tried, she couldn't get the memory of Rory's kiss out of her thoughts. Not pacing, not knitting, not reorganizing, not anything could make her banish that moment to a dusty corner where it belonged.

Plucking the silver frame from the table in the living room, she studied Jack's face. As handsome as her husband was, photographs never seemed capable of capturing his true essence. In the picture, the set to his jaw made him appear rigid and uptight, yet in real life that same expression had made him look determined. Likewise, his hair, which was groomed to perfection in the photograph, bore little resemblance to the way it looked when she mussed it with her hands.

Would a photograph do the ever-present sparkle in Rory's eye justice? And what about that feeling of safety and warmth he exuded? Could *that* be captured in a photograph? She considered the possibility for a split second before it was chased from her thoughts by guilt. What difference did it make how her uncle's employee looked in a picture? He really wasn't her concern.

In the photo, her precious angel was cuddled in Jack's

arms. In contrast to her husband, Natalie looked just as Maggie remembered. Content, peaceful, adorable and oh so very beautiful. Maggie felt a stinging in her eyes as she remembered the silly noise she'd used to elicit that smile on her daughter's face, and how lucky she'd been to keep the camera steady despite the exaggerated hiccup.

She traced the picture with her finger, touching her daughter's wispy hair and surprisingly deep dimples. It was pictures like these that made her hurt most—the ones she'd taken rather than been a part of. Before the accident, she'd treasured them as glimpses in time of the two people she loved most in the world. Since the accident, they made her feel isolated and alone, as if she was a spectator at an event that had been unexpectedly cut short.

But they were all she had now. The pictures and the memories she carried in her head and her heart…

She closed her eyes as she recalled the sensation of Rory's hand on her face, felt the tears forming as she remembered the way he'd moved down to her heart and then her lap. He meant well. He really did. But all his presence did was cloud her thoughts in a way she didn't need or want, reminding her of things she wasn't meant to have.

Setting the frame back on the table, she looked around the room, determined to stay focused on the people that mattered most. For a moment, she contemplated knitting once again, this time making a scarf for her uncle. But the pull simply wasn't strong enough.

No, she needed time with Natalie. Time with her sweet

face, time with her contagious smile, time with her precious little fingers and toes...

The journal.

Maggie spun around, hurrying toward her bedroom and the coat and purse she'd flung on the nightstand before dissolving into tears. There was a part of her that felt a little guilty for allowing such a wonderful night to become overshadowed by reality. But it was the other guilt—the all-encompassing guilt—that told her to let it go. The less she saw Rory O'Brien, the better.

She pushed her coat and purse to the side, but found nothing underneath. "Where on earth—" She stopped as thoughts of her sudden departure from Rory's home flooded her.

Uh-oh. She'd left her journal behind.

A wave of disappointment washed over her. She couldn't ask for it back without seeing him again. And *that* she couldn't risk.

She'd had her second chance in life.

And just like that, the memory of Rory's kiss was gone, in its place a sense of loss so profound she actually ached. She needed to *do* something, to spend time with her daughter....

The leaf.

Recalling their mommy-and-me outing to the zoo once again, she sat on the edge of the bed and reached for the memory box she'd set on the nightstand the evening she arrived at the inn. With careful hands she removed the lid and set it aside, her attention moving to the jumbled contents she hadn't had the heart to look at in entirely too long.

One by one she lifted them out, turned every item over and over in her hands, savoring the past.

A soft sound outside the door of her suite made her freeze. Her attention was diverted toward the living room as a white square slid across the floor.

Wanting to be alone with her memories, she considered ignoring it, the identity of the person behind it all but certain. But a letter or a note wasn't *him*. And the sooner she looked at whatever it was, the sooner she could get back to what really mattered.

Tentatively, she made her way over to the note. Reaching down, she snatched it off the floor and opened it, her eyes soaking in the masculine handwriting that was scrawled across the single sheet of paper.

Maggie,
I enjoyed your company this evening. You brought a warmth into my home that was both welcomed and appreciated. Thank you, for that.

You left your journal behind. And I, in turn, have left it outside your door. I hope it brings you some peace.
Rory

An inexplicable shiver ran down her spine, leaving a sense of loneliness in its wake. There was no doubt about it, Rory was a nice man. A special one, even. But he couldn't be her concern. Not now. Not ever.

She read the letter once again, the loneliness morphing into a sense of purpose that propelled her toward the front door. Sure enough, the leather-bound journal with gold trim was just where he had said.

Opening it, she allowed her fingers to flip through the pages, her mind filling in the blanks with the memories she wanted to record.

HE TOSSED HIS KEYS onto the end table and sank into the cushions of his couch. The urge to approach her in the hallway as she'd bent to retrieve the journal had been intense. But so had been the little voice that had warned him off.

It broke his heart to see Maggie allowing herself a moment of happiness, only to stamp on it with her own two feet, convinced that love and loss went hand in hand.

He understood it more than she realized. The feelings he struggled with where his brother was concerned weren't much different. Only instead of begrudging himself happiness, he blamed himself for things he couldn't undo.

Maggie, on the other hand, was a different story. It wasn't too late with her. She was hurting *now*. And he knew it. Her pain was raw and ever-present, just as Reardon's had been.

Glancing up at the tree, Rory gazed at the wishing ball, a symbol of hope calling to him like a beacon in a storm. He sat up straight, a swirl of ideas hitting him with a one-two punch.

"I can make seasonal wall hangings…and I've toyed with personalizing picture frames—you know, for special occasions."

Doing things with his hands always made him feel productive, giving him an accomplishment to take pride in. It was at those times he was able to hold the guilt at bay and actually cut himself a break.

Perhaps the same would work for Maggie.

Which got him thinking. About a conversation he'd had at the gift shop where he'd bought the journal. The woman behind the counter had encouraged him to come back to take advantage of the sales related to her upcoming move out-of-state.

The shop had been busy, with customers standing in line to purchase a variety of items to better their life and their home. It was a perfect place for such a store, thanks to a high number of vacationers during the spring and summer months.

Was that something Maggie could do? Especially when she had the ability to make much of the inventory herself?

It was a solid idea, one that excited him more and more with each passing moment. But it was also an idea that needed Maggie's active participation, something he doubted he'd get without a fight.

Unless, of course, he shoved first and asked later.

Chapter Nine

Maggie tossed and turned, her face brushing against the dampened pillow again and again, her mind locked in a dream she couldn't shut off. It was a dream she'd had often. Yet this time there was a sound—a staccato tapping she didn't remember.

Had the truck driver knocked on the window before retrieving her from underneath the car?

The tapping grew louder.

Had she smacked the window to get out?

The tapping morphed into a pounding sound that startled her awake. She bolted upright, her gaze coming to rest on the journal she'd worked on all night. Still open to Natalie's First Christmas, the book was surrounded by colorful pens, spools of delicate ribbon and scraps from cut photographs.

A smile tugged at her lips, until she heard again that pounding from her dream.

"Maggie, are you there? Please, Maggie, I need to know you're okay."

Rory.

Had it been him knocking all that time? She glanced

at the clock, noted the late morning hour. If Natalie were alive, Maggie would have been up hours ago—singing songs, reading storybooks and playing with shape sorters, building blocks and baby dolls....

"Maggie?"

She considered ignoring his knock, but the concern in his voice pulled at something inside her chest. He was worried. Scared, even. She knew what that was like, knew what it was to call for someone again and again, only to hear nothing in response.

Swinging her legs over the edge of the bed, she slipped her feet into the well-worn pink slippers she'd tossed in her suitcase at the last minute, the aging footwear one of only a handful of items she'd opted to bring when she left Missouri. Other than a few pictures, her clothes and her box of mementos, nothing else had really mattered.

A click echoed through the suite, followed by the sound of footsteps. She peered out into the living room, her eyes widening at the sight of Rory O'Brien standing in the middle of her living room, a key clenched in his fist.

"What are you doing in here?" she asked, her voice rising in anger, only to fade as images from their evening together flooded her mind. He was clad now in a pair of faded blue jeans and an oatmeal-colored shirt that hugged his arms in all the right places, his very presence jettisoning her back to the sofa in his living room and the way he'd held her close as they'd kissed.

He held up his hands. "I'm sorry. I really am. But I started knocking twenty minutes ago. At first I thought you weren't answering because you couldn't hear me, so

I knocked louder. Then I thought you were ignoring me, and figured I should just leave. But when I remembered why I'd come, I decided to give it one more shot. And that's when I got nervous. You were so…I don't know… *detached* last night when you left that I was afraid maybe you'd—" He stopped, took a long slow inhale and then shrugged. "I'm sorry, Maggie. I was just worried, and I couldn't stand by and do nothing. Not this time."

It was hard to stay angry at someone who was only trying to do the right thing. She opened her mouth to let him off the hook, then closed it just as fast as his attention clearly dropped from her face to her powder-blue silk camisole and matching shorts.

"I'm sorry. Were…were you sleeping?" he asked as he deliberately raised his eyes upward once again. The look of hunger she saw in them was unmistakable.

She shrugged, the motion causing one of her straps to slip down her arm. His eyes followed. "I guess you could call it sleeping. I think I heard you knocking, but thought it was…" With a wave of her hand, she steered the topic from a path she simply didn't want to venture down. "Anyway, it's okay. I shouldn't have been sleeping this late. But since I didn't finish until nearly seven this morning, I guess I crashed."

"That's good, right?"

"I suppose." She willed her focus off the man in front of her, forced it onto *anything* other than him…and his arms…and the taste of his lips….

Maggie reached across the bed, grabbed hold of the journal and tugged it toward her. "Would you like to see what I did?"

"Absolutely."

Perching on the edge of the mattress, she patted the spot next to her as she once again lost herself in the pages she'd created throughout the night. "This is my Natalie," she whispered as Rory's leg grazed hers. "See?"

He leaned a little closer. "Oh, wow…Maggie, she's beautiful."

Maggie beamed. "She is, isn't she? And what a sweet, sweet disposition she had. Once she figured out how to smile, she never stopped."

He leaned still closer. "Her chin and her smile are the spitting image of yours."

"You really think so?" Maggie stared at the little face that hovered in her thoughts morning, noon and night. "I always thought she smiled more like Jack."

"I didn't know your husband, so I can't comment as to whether there was a similarity, but trust me, that smile is yours." Rory looked up from the book and studied her closely. "And just like yours, it's breathtaking."

Feeling her face grow warm, Maggie rushed to change the subject, keenly aware of Rory's thigh against hers.

She flipped to the front of the album, to the page that started it all. "This is the day she was born. She came bright and early, just as the sun was starting to rise." Pointing toward the upper right corner of the page, Maggie couldn't help but sigh. "See her little footprint? Wasn't it tiny?"

He leaned forward for a closer look, his nearness making her heart flutter.

"Wow. Her whole foot wasn't much bigger than my big toe."

She turned to the next page. "And this was the day she came home from the hospital."

"Is that wallpaper?" he asked.

"Not exactly." She tapped her finger on the photograph of Natalie's nursery that showed the border stencil Maggie had created around the room. "It's really just a slip of paper I used to make sure I didn't mess up the real thing."

He stared at her. "You painted those teddy bears?"

"I used a stencil. But a stencil I'd created." She looked again at the piece of paper where she'd practiced the bears' facial expressions in order to get the shading just right. "You probably think I'm silly, saving a piece of scrap paper, huh?"

"Nah, I'd have done the same thing."

She opened her eyes. "Really?"

He nodded. "I'm a sucker for that kind of stuff. Which explains why my spare bedroom looks the way it does."

"I don't understand."

"It's filled with boxes. And I do mean boxes. Most of it is stuff from my parents' house after they passed away. Delilah says I should have an estate sale, and I guess on some level I know she's right. But it's hard to let it go. I mean, I flipped through those books as a kid, I used that silverware throughout my entire childhood, I—" He stopped, his face turning crimson. "Wow. I must sound like an idiot."

Maggie laughed. "No. Not at all. It makes you even more..." Realizing what she was about to say, she stopped and changed course, turning their attention back to the book in her hands. "Once I got the pictures and the keepsakes where I wanted them on each page, I wrote a paragraph or two about that particular day."

"May I?" he asked, as he pointed toward the book, a smile curving his lips.

She nodded in assent.

But as he leaned close once again, she couldn't help but second-guess her decision. Especially now, with the memory of his kiss still so raw.

Scooting back so as to lessen their proximity, she couldn't help but feel the unfamiliar pull somewhere deep inside her soul. A pull that countered everything her head was saying.

Sure, he was good-looking. Extremely good-looking, if she allowed herself a moment of honesty. And he was thoughtful beyond comparison. Bringing her the journal despite her rudeness was proof of that.

Her rudeness...

She looked down at the back of his head as he continued to read, her hands virtually itching to touch him. Just once...

Instead, she willed herself to pay close attention to the words that suddenly poured from her mouth. "Rory? I'm sorry about last night...about leaving a nice evening on such a negative note. But—" she swallowed as he sat up to look at her, momentarily throwing her off her game "—but mostly...I—I'm sorry for kissing you the way I did. I had no business doing that."

For a moment it was there in his eyes—a disappointment so raw, so vivid, that it nearly broke her heart. Then, just as fast as it appeared, it was gone, in its place a look so compassionate, so full of understanding and concern for her that she couldn't speak another word.

"I'm sorry, too. I should have known you weren't ready."

She looked down at the precious pictures of her daughter. "I'll never be ready," she whispered.

His hand covered hers and squeezed ever so gently. "You will be. One day. When the right man comes along. And you'll know it when he does. He'll make you laugh. He'll give you hope. He'll make you catch your breath. And he'll creep into your thoughts when you least expect it. Because that's what the right one does."

Make her laugh? Give her hope? Creep his way into her thoughts?

She sucked in her breath as an unexpected realization struck. That was exactly the way she felt about—

Rory.

HE GRABBED FOR the journal as she leaped to her feet, her movement so sudden, so unexpected that it nearly knocked him off the bed. "Whoa. Did I say something wrong?" he asked, hanging on to the mattress with one hand and the journal with the other.

She whirled around to face him, the silky straps of her pajama top slipping still farther down her shoulders.

He swallowed. Hard.

Even with that look of unexplained horror on her face, Maggie was still one of the most beautiful women he'd ever seen. And the red-rimmed eyes she'd sported when he'd first arrived? They just made him want to pull her close and protect her from all the hard parts of life.

"I'm going to have to ask you to leave," she said, her slipper-clad feet moving in the direction of the living room. "I—I'm not feeling very well right now."

"Are you sick?" he asked. Carefully, he placed the journal on the bed, then joined her in the main room. "It's awfully cold in here and wearing those slippers on a cold wood floor certainly doesn't help."

"My slippers are fine." Her hands found her hips in record fashion.

"Well, you must admit they've seen better days."

"You're right. They have."

He cocked his head to the side and studied her, the double meaning behind her words not lost on him. "For now…maybe. But that doesn't negate the fact that the floor is cold. And so is this whole room." Bypassing her, he strode over to the fireplace and plucked a log from the holder. "Let me make a fire for you, okay? It's the least I can do after barging in on you the way that I did."

"You were worried. I get that."

"Terrified is more like it." He turned to face her one more time, felt his breath hitch at the unexpected look in her eyes. Not sure what to say, he dropped to his knees beside the grate and shoved a few logs into the hearth. "This'll just take a minute. Then I'll be out of your hair."

It's not that he wanted to go, because he didn't. But Maggie no longer wanted him there, he was certain. At least he had been until this moment.

Suddenly he wasn't so sure. Something about what he'd said had struck a nerve. Her reaction was quick and fleeting, but he'd seen it, plain as day. The problem was trying to decipher what it meant and how best to respond.

It was a constant push and pull between his heart and his mind. One he'd experienced all night as he'd pretended to sleep. One minute he'd remember the kiss, his body reacting to the memory in undeniable fashion. Then, just as he'd start to get carried away, he'd remember the pain in her eyes as she'd pulled back.

Maggie was hurting. A deep, penetrating hurt that had seeped into every facet of her life, essentially trapping her in a world from which there was no escape.

What she needed was a life raft. Something to hang on to while she found her footing.

He tossed some kindling onto the logs, then struck a long match, igniting the material with a flick of his wrist. Turning to face her, he offered what he hoped was a nonthreatening smile. "That should help warm things up in here."

"Thank you. But I'd still like to be alone." She shifted from foot to foot, the sadness in her eyes almost more than he could bear.

Throw her a life raft, dude.

A life raft…

"Wait! I have to give you something first." He jogged toward the door and yanked it open, finding the box he'd intended to deliver sitting right where he'd left it when he opted to let himself into her suite with his master key. Lifting it off the floor, he retraced his steps into the living room. "This is why I stopped by. To give you this."

She looked from his face to the box and back again, curiosity pulling her eyebrows upward. "What is that?"

"Just some stuff I found," he lied. "Came across these things in one of the rooms I'm rehabbing. Thought maybe you could find a use for some of it."

"I don't know, Rory. I don't really need any extra stuff. I'm not sure how long I'm going to be staying here, anyway."

Ignoring the last part of her statement, he set the box on the coffee table and gestured to its contents. "Well, just take a look. If you want me to find another home for it, I will. In the meantime, though, I better give you your space." He strode toward the open door, only to stop a few inches from his target. Glancing over his shoulder, he drank in one final look, his gaze lingering on the sleep-tousled hair that cascaded over her bare shoulders like a waterfall.

"Again, I'm sorry for barging in the way I did," he said, taking a final step toward the door. "I just had to know you were okay. And like you, I guess I'm letting my past dictate my present more than it should."

Chapter Ten

Despite what she'd just said, Maggie knew she didn't want Rory to go. Why else did her heart sink at the click of the door? Why else did she feel like running after him and begging him to stay?

"Because you're sick, that's why," she mumbled.

She clapped a hand over her lips as her words registered. Was she? Was she truly having the nervous breakdown her uncle had predicted was on the horizon?

No. She was just trying to find her way. And she would. Eventually.

Eventually has to start sometime, Maggie.

Closing her eyes, she inhaled the sound of Jack's voice, willed it to give her the courage she needed to put one foot in front of the other. Yet, the face that propelled her to actually move from her spot belonged to someone else.

It would start now. Slowly, she made her way over to the box Rory had left behind, the concern in his eyes and the tenderness of his touch playing in her mind as she lifted the flaps and peered inside. Basic wood frames in various shapes and sizes were neatly stacked along one side of the cardboard box. Along the other were bins—colorful plastic containers nested atop one another. She plucked out the top one and opened it to find an assortment of seashells and sand dollars. She grabbed the next few tubs, finding sequins, flat-back faux gemstones, beads and polished stones. The final container held a glue gun, spray adhesive, invisible thread and a large jar of beach sand.

"Who on earth could have left this stuff behind?" she whispered. Leaning back against the sofa, she studied the treasure trove that now covered the coffee table, her creative juices flowing and her mind running in a thousand different directions.

She grabbed a rectangular frame that was designed to house a five-by-eight-inch photograph, and looked at the various bins, her attention stolen by the one containing the seashells. With some beach sand, and a sand dollar or two...

Her mind made up, she searched the room for an empty outlet, plugging the glue gun into the first one she found. Next, she scooped up the supplies she needed and made her way over to the kitchen table, its clear surface a testament to the fact she'd eaten nothing more than apples since arriving.

Well, apples and a Belgian waffle.

And lasagna...

She bit back the smile that came with both of those memories, and forced her attention onto the project in front of her, remembering to cover the table with a few old newspapers her uncle had left behind. Once her workstation was ready, she uncapped the can of adhesive and sprayed the whole front of the frame. When she was done she sprinkled on some of the beach sand, slowly transforming the basic wood frame into something much more.

Next came the sand dollars. Maggie agonized over their placement until she was sure she'd found just the right spots, cementing her decision with the help of the hot glue. After applying the final shell into place, she scooted back in her chair and admired her work.

"Not bad, if I say so myself."

This time she allowed the smile to come, to lift her mouth in a way that felt more than a little satisfying. She returned to the coffee table and selected a different frame, this time opting to use the invisible thread and bin of colorful beads.

She sat there for hours, decorating one frame after the next until the original pile bore little resemblance to their former selves. When she was done, she simply looked around, a feeling akin to contentment settling over her.

It had been years since she'd tackled a picture frame, even longer since she'd allowed herself to get so caught up by the process that a day would rush by, unnoticed. But once again, she had.

And it felt good. Really, really good.

"In time you'll find a place to put the pain so you can let the joy take over."

She closed her eyes, thinking of Delilah's words. Working on the frames, letting her creative energies out, *had* brought Maggie some joy.

Glancing down at the last frame she'd completed, she knew exactly who should have it.

"EXCUSE ME. Is Delilah in today, by any chance?"

The fortysomething redhead looked up from behind the register and stared at Maggie as if she had two heads. "That's kinda like asking whether McDonald's has hamburgers."

Feeling suddenly foolish, Maggie clasped the handles of the gift bag tighter and shrugged. "I'm sorry. I didn't know. It's only my second time in here. As an adult, anyway."

The woman's expression softened. "Hey, don't mind me. I was supposed to have the night off for a date. But the clown stood me up. So I figured I'd come in and make a little money instead." Standing, the redhead extended her hand. "I'm Virginia."

"I'm Maggie. Maggie Monroe." Shifting the bag, she shook hands with a smile. "Do you think I could have a moment with your boss? I have something I'd like to give her."

"Sure thing. But it could take a moment. She's in back planning her pies for tomorrow."

"Her pies?"

Virginia nodded. "The process is similar, I imagine, to the one scientists go through when they're trying to figure out what gene to study next." The woman stepped from behind the counter and indicated Maggie should follow. "So would you like to have a seat for a few moments? I could bring you something to drink while you're waiting. Maybe a hot coffee or something?"

"Make it a hot chocolate and you've got yourself a deal. It's freezing out there," she said, trailing the woman to a booth not far from the door.

"Welcome to Lake Shire, Michigan." Virginia stepped to the side, allowing Maggie access to the booth, and then plunked a menu down in front of her. "Just in case you're hungry. You *are* in Delilah's place, you know."

Maggie couldn't help but laugh. "Oh, trust me, I know."

Virginia looked over her shoulder before leaning close to Maggie's ear. "If you ask me, her beef stew is the best thing on the menu. Well…that and the caramel pie."

Maggie's stomach rumbled, an increasingly familiar sound she knew was a good sign. If nothing else, it meant the notion of food was no longer taboo.

Virginia nodded knowingly. "I got you with the caramel pie, didn't I?"

"I think you did. Though, in all honesty, the mention of beef stew jettisoned me back to my grandma's kitchen." She tugged off her gloves and set them on the table, her attention momentarily diverted by the miniature Christmas tree poised on the ledge. The star ornaments that dangled from it branches held various sayings.

Never stop dreaming.

Reach for the stars.

Hope.

"That tree is my favorite. Not sure if it's because it's the newest of the bunch or because I like the little lift those words give me." Virginia cleared her throat. "As for the stew…no offense to your grandma, but there's no stew in this entire world that's better than Delilah's. Just doesn't exist."

Maggie's stomach rumbled again. On a whim, she pushed the menu back across the table, her mind made up. "I'll take a small bowl of the stew."

"A small? You sure?" Scooping up the menu, Virginia conducted an all-too-obvious inspection of Maggie— from her ponytail to the dark denim jeans she'd tucked into soft leather boots.

She nodded, wiggling out of her charcoal-gray parka as she did. "A small works."

"A small it is." Virginia took a step back, then stopped. "And a hot chocolate, right?"

"Right. And Delilah, too, when she's free."

"And Delilah, too, when she's free," the woman repeated, before disappearing through a swinging door near the back of the diner.

Once she was gone, Maggie looked back at the tree, her gaze settling on the last ornament she'd seen.

Hope.

"Hope," she repeated to herself, the sound of the word making her sit upright. Hope was what she'd felt the last time she was here. Hope was what she'd felt while knitting alongside Delilah. And hope was what she'd felt while making the picture frames.

The fact that two of the three were connected to Rory in some way made her pause before willing herself to read more of the ornaments.

Hope is the spark that ignites dreams.

She stared at the last one.

Without hope there is no joy.

Was that why she was finding it harder and harder to harness Natalie's joy? Because she'd let hope die along with her daughter?

The thought was sobering. And more than a little eye-opening.

"Maggie, what a wonderful surprise!"

Her head snapped upward. "Delilah, hi!"

Wiping her hands on the cloth napkin wedged inside her apron strings, the robust woman with the warm eyes smiled from deep inside. "Hi, yourself. I hope you're here to eat."

She laughed. "Actually, I wasn't. But Virginia is rather persuasive."

Grinning broadly, Delilah slid onto the empty bench across from her. "And that's exactly why I give her hours whenever she wants them. She's good for the cash box."

"I can see that." Maggie cast one more look in the direction of the little tree and its ornaments, and then placed the gift bag on the table. "I brought you something."

"Whatever for?" Delilah asked in surprise. "It's not my birthday."

"It's not supposed to be. This is for taking time out of your busy schedule to teach me to knit."

The woman reached for the bag and then stopped. "You took to it like a duck to water, from what I saw."

"We just practiced stitches."

"And then you made a scarf. A very good one."

She peered at her new friend. "How did you know I made a scarf?"

Delilah pulled the bag closer. "Because he couldn't

have been any prouder. He showed it to practically everyone in the diner when he stopped by that afternoon. Heck, he even showed it off in the parking lot on the way to his truck."

Maggie felt her mouth gape open. "Rory did?"

"Did you make a scarf for anyone else?" Without waiting for a reply, the woman reached into the gift bag and pulled out the beaded frame, her own mouth dropping open. "Oh Maggie...it's beautiful. Absolutely beautiful. Where on earth did you find this?"

Shaking her head free of the sudden barrage of Rory-related images, she willed herself to follow the shift in topic. "I made it," she said.

Delilah looked up from the frame. "You *made* this?"

She nodded.

"Really?"

She nodded again.

"Maggie, I don't know what to say!"

"Don't. It's my way of saying thank-you. For teaching me something I've always wanted to learn."

"It was my pleasure." Delilah turned the frame over and thrust it in her direction, followed by a pen. "Would you sign the back for me?"

"Sign the back? Are you serious?"

"It'll be neat to say I knew you before you got all famous."

She couldn't help but laugh at the absurdity of that statement. "Famous? It's just a picture frame, Delilah."

"There's nothing *just* about this, Maggie. You could

make a lot of money with these kinds of things. Especially in a vacation town like this one."

"You really think so?" she asked, the woman's words an echo of a sentiment she'd heard expressed in this very diner not more than three days earlier.

"I really *know* so." Delilah looked up as Virginia approached the table with Maggie's stew. "Perfect timing. I have to get back into the kitchen and finish my pie choices." She turned to Maggie. "Take your time with the stew. I'll be back to visit in a few minutes."

Virginia set the bowl on the table in front of her. "Oh, my…that's lovely," she said as she pointed at the frame. "Where did that come from? I have to have one."

"Maggie made it. For me."

"You made this? Seriously?"

Again Maggie nodded, an unfamiliar sense of pride enveloping her.

"How much do you charge?"

"How much do I charge?" she repeated. "I don't—"

"Twenty-five bucks," Delilah interjected.

"Delilah, I don't—"

"I'll take one." Virginia lifted the frame from the table and studied it closely. "Do you think you could make mine with different shades of blue?" She shot a look in her boss's direction. "That would look real nice in my living room, don't you think?"

"It would look perfect," Delilah agreed.

Maggie started to protest, to offer to make one for her free of charge, but Delilah's hand shot out, cutting her off.

"When can you have it ready?" Virginia asked. "I

have some company coming into town just after New Year's and I'd love to have it by then if possible."

"I, uh…"

"That gives you nearly five weeks, dear. You can surely do that, right?" Delilah prodded.

"I, uh…" she repeated, before looking back at the tree. The answer left her mouth before she realized what she was saying. "Sure. I can have it for you by then."

Virginia clapped her hands together. "Ohh, I'm so excited. Getting stood up this evening wasn't so bad, after all." Not waiting for an answer, she pulled a napkin-wrapped bundle of flatware from her apron pocket. "Enjoy your stew. I promise you won't be sorry. It's the best—oh…hey there, Rory, how are you this evening?"

At the sound of his name, Maggie turned in her seat, her attention riveted on the handsome man in the black henley and faded denim jeans standing not more than a foot away from her booth.

She swallowed.

"Better now," he replied, his gaze meeting hers as he leaned over and planted a kiss on Delilah's cheek. "I was hoping you might have some stew lying around for me, too."

"For two of my favorite people? Of course. Virginia, can you set another place for Rory?"

"I don't want to barge in on Maggie's dinner. I'll just sit over there by the—"

Buoyed by the events of the day, she waved her hand. "No, please. I'd enjoy the company."

Surprise lit his eyes, only to be chased away by a smile

that carved those unforgettable dimples in his cheeks. "You sure?" he asked softly.

She glanced at the frame now clutched in Delilah's hand, a long-lost feeling beginning to resurface in some dusty recess of her heart. "I'm sure."

Chapter Eleven

He couldn't help but notice the difference in her face—the hint of a sparkle in her dark brown eyes, the upward tilt to her mouth, her relaxed shoulders. It was the Maggie he'd had glimpses of all week, yet this time it seemed less fleeting.

"You look great, Maggie. Really great." Her sheer presence was creating nothing short of a magnetic pull where his body was concerned. Her hair, which normally hung down her back, had been arranged in a high ponytail, just as it had been the last time they'd been at the diner together, the playful style both adorable and sexy at the same time.

"Thank you." She removed her flatware from the paper napkin Virginia had left behind, her long slender fingers laying everything just so beside her bowl. When she was done, she draped the napkin across her lap and simply sat there, waiting.

"Aren't you going to eat that?" he asked.

"When yours arrives."

"No. It'll get cold. Please, start without me."

Instead of complying, she pointed toward the tree.

"Did you see this one? It's even better than the one we had at our table last time."

He leaned closer, reading the words on the star-shaped ornaments. "Wow...look at that. I've never seen anything like that before."

Scooting to the right just a little, Maggie slipped her hand behind a sparkly silver star and turned it so he could see.

"'Hope is the spark that ignites dreams,'" he read aloud. "That's a good one. And it's so true."

"I didn't realize how true until today."

"Why's that? Did something happen today?"

"I'll say." She propped her elbows on the edge of the table and rested her chin on her hands, the end of her ponytail cascading down the front of her shoulder.

"Tell me."

"It has to do with that box you dropped off this morn-ing. The one you found in one of the empty rooms."

"Yes?"

"Well, it had everything you could possibly imagine for decorating picture frames. There were beads and sequins and seashells and sand and glue and wire." She stopped, her eyes shining with an excitement he found more than a little alluring. "I mean, remember how I told you the other night about my personalized picture—"

She stared at him across the table, reality dawning in those big brown eyes he longed to see peering up at him from his bed.

"Wait." Her eyes narrowed. "You didn't just *find* that stuff, did you?"

Uh-oh.

"Did you?" she repeated.

Rubbing a hand across his face, he considered his various options. He could continue the farce, use her uncle as a scapegoat and hope she didn't check his story, or come clean. "Well, I…" Rory stopped, drummed his fingers on the table. "Can I answer that question with another one before I give you your answer?"

A hint of amusement flashed in her eyes as she crossed her arms and waited. "Go ahead."

"Would it affect that smile if I told you I bought it? And just *said* that I found it?"

"In other words, would it bother me if you lied? Is that what you're asking?"

He squirmed in his seat. "'Lie' might be a little strong."

"A little?"

He nodded, the voice in his head berating him for discarding options A and B too quickly.

For a moment she said nothing, her gaze locked with his, her face sporting a look he couldn't quite decipher. But in the end she simply shook her head, causing relief to course through him.

"I don't think anything could affect this smile. But before I explain, I have to ask you why."

"Why what?" he asked, only to be interrupted by Virginia and his bowl of stew. "Mmm, looks and smells heavenly. Thanks, Virginia."

The woman pointed at Maggie. "Did you know about these frames of hers?"

He felt his face warm. "Well, I—"

"I was just yapping to you the other day about needing

knickknacks for my place and you didn't say a thing."
Virginia jabbed a finger into his shoulder. "Do you think
maybe you could have *said* something?"

Confused, he glanced at Maggie. "What's she talking
about?"

"What am I talking about? I'm talking about that
frame she made for Delilah. It's exactly the kind of thing
I'm wanting for my place." Pulling her focus off him, the
waitress planted it squarely on Maggie. "Only for mine,
I want blues galore. Can we do that?"

Maggie fished around inside her purse, coming up
with a small red notebook and a pen. "Absolutely."

"Royal, ocean, that sorta thing. Maybe a navy, too, if
it looks right with the others."

Maggie jotted a few notes, while Rory's confusion
over what was happening remained as strong as ever.

"I'm looking forward to it. Thanks, Virginia."

"No, thank *you*." Virginia wagged a finger in the vi-
cinity of Rory's nose. "Next time, don't be so secretive.
Got it?"

As the woman walked away, he looked back at
Maggie, noting how the happy sparkle in her eyes took
on an air of mischievousness he wouldn't have expected.
"*I'm* being secretive?"

She laughed.

"C'mon. Tell me, would you?"

"Give me a minute. I have to try this first." She pointed
at the stew before dipping her spoon into the thick gravy.
"I have to see whether Virginia is right about this being
the best ever."

"Oh, she's right. Trust me." He sat back in his seat

and simply watched as the curious expression on her face morphed into something close to ecstasy…right down to the I'm-in-heaven eye roll he'd been trying to get Delilah to trademark for more than a few years.

"Well?" he prodded, playfully drumming his fingers on the table.

Maggie said nothing, opting instead for a second, third and fourth spoonful.

"Regretting ordering the small size, aren't you?"

Pausing midbite, she looked across the table at his much larger serving. "Maybe."

He laughed, a deep hearty sound that rumbled in his chest. "Do you *wish* you had more?"

"Maybe," she said, grinning.

He poked his head above the back of the booth. "Virginia? Can we get another small?"

"Comin' right up."

"You didn't have to do that," Maggie whispered as her cheeks reddened.

"Sure I did. You wished for it, didn't you?"

"And what are you…my personal genie?"

"Maybe," he said in a nearly perfect imitation of her voice.

For a moment she said nothing. She simply placed her spoon on the table and scooted back in her seat, silence hovering between them.

A warning bell sounded in his head. He'd done it again. He'd pushed just a little too hard. "Look, Maggie, I'm sorry. It's just that I like to—"

She cut his apology off midsentence. "I'm not upset. I'm just…touched."

He braced himself for a moment, waiting for the inevitable shoe to drop, but it didn't happen. Instead, she simply continued, her words giving him the first burst of real hope he'd felt where she was concerned.

"I suppose, deep inside, I knew you had to have put that box together on your own. But I wasn't really thinking about how it got there or why it got there. Then, when I opened it, something inside me clicked. Something that I haven't felt in months." Lifting a piece of bread to her lips, she took a tiny bite. She seemed to be eating much more easily than she had the other day, and for that he was pleased. "The next thing I knew, four hours had passed and I'd decorated every frame in the box."

"Every frame?" he repeated.

"Every frame." She looked across at him rather sheepishly. "I know I should have paced myself better but—"

"The creativity took over, huh?"

"Yes! In a way it hasn't in entirely too long."

So he'd been right….

"I'm glad, Maggie. I was kind of hoping that would happen."

She stared at him. "But how did you know? How did you know I'd react that way?"

"I didn't for sure. But I had hope…because that's what my work does for me," he explained. "When I'm working in one of the rooms at the inn, I feel productive. I can lose myself in the process of making something whole again—making it even better than it was in the beginning."

Bending forward, she ate a bit more of her stew before

responding. "I don't want you to think I didn't enjoy the knitting lesson, because I did. But that was about learning something new. This? This was about taking a step forward."

"How so?"

"I was able to immerse myself in something from my past that didn't make me feel as if I'd lost something. It was like a reminder."

"A reminder of what?"

"That I'm still here. The same Maggie I've always been, with the same interests and the same passions I've always had." She set her spoon down and reached across the table, her hand meeting his halfway. "And I'll be honest, there's a part of me that wants to take those words back…to fight the idea of having anything that resembles a life. But there's also a part that wants to embrace it."

"Listen to that second part," he said, savoring the gentle squeeze she gave before pulling her hand back across the table.

"Most of the time all I can see is what I've lost. And when I stack that against anything I might still have, the latter just doesn't matter."

"Then *don't* stack it, Maggie. Because it's different. There's a good and a bad everywhere. I mean, look at Delilah. She's devoted her life to this diner. So much so that she doesn't really have much else." He considered trying to reach for Maggie's hand again, but discarded the notion in favor of keeping her focused on what he was saying. Because she needed to hear it. "But the flip side is the fact that she's truly loved here. By everyone—the staff, the customers and just about everyone else in this town."

"I hear what you're saying. I do. But I don't know where to go from here. From the time I was a little girl my only goal was to have my own family again. When I finally found it, I threw myself into it a hundred and fifty percent. Now I'm back to square one."

"But you have another goal now."

"No, I don't."

"You have a dream, don't you? Turn *that* into a goal."

"What dream?"

"The gift shop."

She couldn't help but laugh at the absurdity of his suggestion. "I couldn't do that."

"Of course you could. You'd just need to find a place to lease, make some inventory, lure in customers, that sort of thing."

A small smile appeared on her face. "I *do* already have a customer."

Cocking his head, he studied her closely. "Why do I get this feeling that I'm missing something? First Virginia…and now you?"

Maggie pushed her empty bowl to the side and leaned forward, excitement lighting her eyes. "I brought one of the frames I made to Delilah. That's why I'm here. I wanted to thank her for the knitting lesson."

"Okay…."

"Anyway, Virginia saw the frame I made and went gaga. She loved it so much she's asked me to make her one, too. She asked me how much I charged and when I could get it done by and…" Maggie's words trailed off and a hint of red rose up in her cheeks. "Am I sounding as silly as I think I am?"

"Silly? Are you kidding me? You have a customer. A paying customer. That's awesome!"

She laughed. "Now don't get carried away. It's hardly enough to justify a store."

This time he did reach across the table for her hand, entwining his fingers with hers. "Have you shown your work to anyone else?"

"No."

"Then why assume you can't carry a store? C'mon, think about it. You give Delilah a frame and Virginia sees it and wants one. What happens when she shows it to someone and they want one, too?"

"I don't know."

"I do. You take another one of those steps you've been wanting to take."

"That's a big step."

"Little steps—like eating—morph into slightly bigger steps…like knitting. And then slightly bigger steps move into big giant strides."

"I thought the knitting was a wish."

He smiled. "It was a step disguised as a wish. Or maybe a wish disguised as a step. Either way, it was both."

Virginia reappeared beside the table again, causing Maggie's face to redden as she tugged her hand free.

Confused, Rory looked from her to Virginia and back again. "You okay?" he asked quietly.

She shrugged, then looked up at the waitress.

"Since you liked my stew recommendation so much, I figured you should try one more of Delilah's specialties. On the house, of course." Virginia plunked a plate of caramel pie on the table, followed by a pair of forks.

"What's that?" Maggie asked.

"Delilah's caramel pie," she and Rory answered in unison. "Best in the country."

Once Virginia had moved on to another table, he leaned forward. "Is something wrong? You seemed flustered when Virginia showed up. You don't have to eat the second serving of stew if you're full. Wishes can change when bellies get filled."

She looked down, her expression hard to read. "It's not that. It's just…well, when she showed up, we were holding hands. I don't want her to get the wrong impression."

"The wrong impression?"

Inhaling deeply, she swung her eyes toward the ceiling as if looking for divine intervention. "I think I can actually imagine finding something to pass the time in life— whether that's running a gift shop or not. But giving my heart to someone else? I can't risk that a third time."

He knew the words should come as no surprise. Everything she'd said, everything she'd done from the moment they'd met, had left no room to think otherwise. But still, he hoped for more.

How could he not after the kiss the other night? How could he not when the pictures and the stories she shared showed the kind of woman he'd always wanted?

Resisting the urge to express his thoughts aloud, he did the only thing he could think of to keep her in his life. "You have room for a friend, though, don't you?"

Something flashed across her face—something fleeting, yet undeniable. If he were a betting man, he'd say it was disappointment. But the heart had a funny way of seeing what it wanted to see.

"Because that's what I'd like to be, if you'll let me, Maggie."

SHE COULDN'T REMEMBER a time shopping had ever been so much fun. Or when she'd spent so much money on something that was completely about her.

Hoisting the last of the bags into her trunk, she looked up at Rory, an amused—and slightly dazed—expression on his face. "That was above and beyond the call of friendship, huh?"

"What? Spending an hour walking up and down aisles in an arts-and-crafts store?" He ducked to avoid her playful swat. "A guy can give up his sense of masculinity once in a while. Just so long as it doesn't happen all the time."

"I'm sorry. But I tried to warn you when we left Delilah's." Maggie reached up to shut the trunk, only to have him beat her to the punch. "I told you there wouldn't be a flat-screen television anywhere in the place."

"I figured you had to be mistaken." He laughed. "Seriously, I'm not much of a television guy. And besides, looking at that stuff isn't much different than what I do when I'm getting supplies for my rehab projects."

She stared up at him, noting how the glow from the parking-lot lights made a halo around his face. "How did you get to be so nice?"

"I don't know." He shrugged. "I guess I just wasn't shown how to be any other way."

"You were close to your parents?"

"As close as close could be."

"And…your twin?"

"Inseparable. Until the end, anyway." She touched his gloved hand with hers when his voice faltered.

"Do you miss them?"

"All the time. Though these last few days…not as much."

Pulling the flaps of her coat more tightly against her chest, she exhaled a plume of frosty air. "W-why? W-w-why not as much the last few days?" she asked with chattering teeth.

He grabbed hold of her arm, his sudden nearness making her throat tighten and her body tingle. "Let's get in the car. We can talk on the way back to Delilah's."

With a shiver, she agreed, slipping behind the steering wheel in time to watch him walk around the hood of the car. She couldn't help but notice the confident way he moved or the admiring looks he drew from more than a few women in the parking lot.

He shut the passenger-side door, picking up their conversation where he'd left off. "You asked why I haven't missed them as much the last few days, right?"

She nodded, finding that the sound of his voice in such tight quarters stirred something inside her she couldn't quite identify. It wasn't fear—she trusted him in a way she couldn't begin to describe, let alone understand. It wasn't sadness—she'd had more fun in the past few hours than she'd had since…well, since the last time they were together. It wasn't nerves—

Or was it?

Suddenly she felt like a high-school girl alone with the boy she'd had a crush on all year.

Only she wasn't a high-school kid. And she couldn't have a crush on Rory….

"I haven't missed them as much lately because I've had someone else on my mind. Someone special."

He's just a friend. Someone to talk to. Someone to eat with once in a while.

"You see, since my brother died, I've kept to myself more or less. I've gone on a date or two, but nothing more than that. Most of the time—when I wasn't working—I simply preferred to stay home. With my guilt and my memories. Then one day I agreed to do a favor for someone I respect more than I can ever say. And, well, I did it. And the moment the door opened, my world changed."

The moment the door opened…

What was he saying? She tried to focus on the words pouring from his lips, but instead found herself remembering the way those same lips had felt on hers….

"Now I'm not so inundated by my own problems."

Distracted, she looked into Rory's eyes, losing herself in their clear blue depths. Leaning across the center console, she grasped his chin with her thumb and index finger and tugged it downward toward her mouth.

"Maggie, are you sure? I don't want to do anything to—"

"I'm sure," she whispered back, shutting her eyes as he closed the gap between them.

An instant later their lips met and their tongues mingled as he cupped the back of her head with one hand and gently touched the side of her face with his other. Snaking her arms around his neck, she yielded to the intensity growing between them, an intensity she knew he felt every bit as much as she did.

Slowly, yet deliberately, his hand left her face, traveled down her jawline to her neck, the feel of his fingers on her bare skin only deepening the desire that made her body yearn for his in a way she'd never experienced before.

Chapter Twelve

She didn't remember much about the drive back to the diner. Or how he'd gotten out of her car and into his own. But she remembered the kiss.

And she remembered it well.

The way his lips tasted, the way he'd touched her face, the way he'd stroked her hair and held her close afterward...

Tossing her keys onto the small table beside the door, Maggie walked into her suite at the inn, her attention drawn to the bare tree in front of the picture window that overlooked Lake Shire. It wasn't a big tree, but it was pretty. Or could be, if she dressed it up a bit.

Only instead of hanging the ornaments that had so many memories attached to them, maybe she could make new ones. After all, if she was going to consider the notion of owning a gift shop one day, having a ready-made supply of ornaments to go with the frames she'd made would be a smart move.

Her mind made up, she headed into her bedroom toward the box of craft supplies she'd brought with her on the drive from Missouri. Every button, every bead, every piece of wire, every piece of wood, every can of paint she'd left untouched since before Natalie was born was right where she'd put it, in color-coded bins. It was the only box she'd stuffed in the car that didn't have a connection to Jack and Natalie. And the only reason she'd packed it had been because of her uncle.

Somehow, some way, it was as if he'd known its contents would be the bridge she needed, just as he seemed to know books and quiet moments together were what she'd needed as a heartbroken child.

She hoisted the box into her arms and carried it out to the living room, setting it beside the items she'd purchased with Rory. Leaving Missouri had been easier than she would have imagined, with Natalie's too-quiet nursery and Jack's darkened office transforming her home into a place she no longer recognized or wanted.

The money from the sale was tucked away in the bank, waiting for her to decide what path to take in life. And now, thanks to Rory, she had a glimpse of what her future could be.

Rummaging through the box of wooden shapes, she extracted a medium-size heart. Eyeing it carefully, she imagined how it would look painted red with a white lace, scalloped border, and perhaps a message written in the center with a silver glitter pen.

As she worked, she found herself so engrossed that she thought of little else. She painted, she stitched, she glued, and she hummed one Christmas carol after the next until she found the one she wanted to vary to fit her first ornament.

Gripping the silver glitter pen she wrote: **Have yourself a mistletoe Christmas.**

Satisfied, she leaned back to study the finished project, the calligraphy's graceful loops lending itself to the
whimsical feel she'd set out to create.

"A mistletoe Christmas," she read aloud as her
thoughts returned to Rory's lips. Never in her wildest
dreams could she ever have imagined a kiss like his. It
had been sweet in its tenderness, exciting in its passion,
and more than a little memorable.

And then, just like that, she found herself wishing for
a sprig of mistletoe to hang in the suite. Perhaps above
the front door? Or maybe in the doorway to the tiny
kitchen?

The ring of the phone pulled her back to the moment,
the repeating sound leading her to the bedroom. Plopping
herself down on the bed, she reached for the receiver.
"Hello?"

"It's Rory."

She sucked in her lower lip, releasing it along with
the smile his voice created. "Hi."

"I just wanted to make sure you got home okay."

"I did. I've been working ever since."

"On Virginia's frame?"

Maggie swiveled on the bed, pulling her legs onto
the mattress and snuggling into the mound of pillows.
"Would you believe ornaments?"

"Ornaments?" he echoed.

"I don't know…I guess it finally hit me how pathetic
my tree looks. So I figured I'd make a few."

"You're going to decorate?"

"Well, sorta. And besides, they'll come in handy in case—" She stopped, unsure whether she'd sound like an idiot if she admitted to the notion of building up a supply of items for a shop she didn't have.

"In case you want to sell them along with your frames?"

She gripped the phone tighter. "How did you know?"

His smile was audible across the line. "So then I'm right?"

"Yes," she finally confessed. "Rather silly of me, don't you think?"

"Wishes and dreams are never silly. Unless you ignore them."

"Do you ever ignore yours?"

"I did when I was working behind a desk. But once I realized that…once I admitted it to myself…I made a change."

"Made a change," she repeated in a whisper.

"Maggie? You still there?"

She nodded.

"Maggie?"

"Uh, yeah, I'm still here. I guess I'm just thinking about what you said." She glanced over at the pile of frames she'd decorated earlier. "You know, about dreams and wishes. And, well, I guess I'm wondering if I should go ahead and do it."

"Is it something you want?" he asked, his voice warm and masculine.

"I think it might be."

"What are you doing tomorrow?"

She looked back at the ceiling. "Tomorrow? Why?"

"I want to show you something. Something I think you might be interested in."

"Can you give me a hint?"

For a moment he said nothing, his silence an unwelcome sound in her ears. Without Maggie realizing it, Rory O'Brien had become important to her—his presence a lifeline of sorts in a life that had become much too big and much too lonely. The relief that swept through her when he finally spoke only served to underscore that reality.

"I'll concede you one word. But that's it, okay?"

She laughed. "Okay. Go."

"Think *genie*."

"Who's Jeannie?"

"I said one word. That's it. So…how about I pick you up around ten-thirty?"

She feigned irritation. "I'm supposed to agree to this knowing nothing more than *Jeannie?*"

"That's right."

It felt good to laugh, the feeling it evoked not much different than the first burst of sun after a deluge of rainy days. The warmth lifted her spirits and gave her courage to face another day.

A day with an actual plan…

"I'll be ready at ten-thirty."

RORY REACHED FOR THE phone book the second she hung up, the dial tone in his ear an acceptable sound this one time. Under any other circumstances, he'd have done just about anything he could think of to prolong their conversation, the sound of her sweet voice doing things to his body he wasn't ready to have end.

But these weren't normal circumstances.

He had a plan. One he needed to enact now before it got any later.

Flipping the book open to the yellow pages in the center, he quickly found the heading he was looking for. Then, after a quick skim of the names listed underneath, he dialed.

Chapter Thirteen

He tucked the ornament behind his back as the door swung open, the sight of Maggie's sweet brown eyes chasing the chill from his body.

"Oh, my gosh, you look like a giant ice cube." She reached into the hallway and pulled him inside the suite. "Come in, come in."

Stepping forward, he willed his teeth to keep from chattering. "It's not too bad. Just a little nippy is all."

"A little nippy?" she asked as her left eyebrow shot upward. "Your lips are practically blue."

"You could warm them up." The second the words were out he wished he could recall them. It was too soon to tease like that. And certainly too soon to assume their kiss from the other night was something she wanted to repeat.

Even if he did…a million times over.

She pointed at the hand he was hiding. "What do you have?"

Saved by the wishing ball…

He pulled out the familiar red box and held it toward her. "You said you were going to decorate your tree, after all, so I figured you should have this back." He watched as her gaze left his face and settled on the box. "Granted, it's not one you made, but it's one your uncle wanted you to have."

For a moment he thought she was going to protest, but in the end, she took it from him. "All right. I'll hang it. But I'm not ready to write anything on one of those slips."

"That's okay. It has the wish I wrote. It can wait for one from you for as long as it takes." He touched the collar of his coat. "Notice the scarf?"

A smile swept across her face. "I did."

"You made it."

"I know that."

"Just figured I'd point it out. In case you forgot."

"Then what's your excuse for telling everyone at the diner? And in the parking lot outside?"

His face grew warm. "Um, I—well, hmm. Did I do that?"

"Delilah said you did."

"That woman has very loose lips at times." He glanced at the floor and then back at Maggie, the sparkle of amusement in her eyes warming him in a way that was completely unrelated to getting in out of the cold. "What? She does! Ask anyone. They'll all tell you the same thing. Lovable, yes. But able to keep her mouth shut? Uh, no."

Maggie rolled her eyes skyward, then spun around and moved toward the tree, her graceful hips swaying in hypnotic fashion. "This ornament is so beautiful I'm almost afraid it's going to make the rest of them look silly in comparison."

"Rest of them?" he asked as he followed. "I don't see any other ornaments."

"I'm making them. One at a time." She pulled the wishing ball from the box and held it for a moment. "None of them are this exquisite."

"How many have you made so far?" He searched the branches and came up empty.

"Just one." Rising up on tiptoe, she placed the ball on a branch near the top, dead center.

"Where is it?"

She pointed toward the table in the far corner of the room. "Over there. I haven't hung it yet."

With several long strides he was across the room, staring down at a beautifully painted heart-shaped ornament. "You made this?"

"Yes."

He studied it closely, noting the lace border and the handwritten inscription across the center. "'Have yourself a *mistletoe* Christmas'?"

When she didn't respond, he glanced up, saw the way she shifted from foot to foot, nibbling her lower lip as she did. "What's wrong? It's great."

Her shoulders slumped with obvious relief. "Really?"

"Absolutely. In fact, I think it's the kind of thing that'll sell fast. Real fast."

"You don't think it's goofy?"

He looked back at the ornament, read it a second time. "Why would I think that?"

"I don't know. I guess I just assumed most people wouldn't get my fascination with mistletoe."

"Fascination?"

She nodded. "I used to hide behind the couch when I was a little girl and watch my father kiss my mother under the mistletoe every night. He would find ways to get her to meet him in that exact spot. He'd drop something there and wait for her to pick it up, or pretend to show her something and just happen to be standing right there when he asked her to come see it—you know, that sort of thing. Looking back, I suspect she knew what he was up to all along, but she never let on."

Rory couldn't help but laugh. "And they didn't know you were spying on them from behind the couch?"

"I don't know. They never said. But I don't think it mattered. They loved each other. And they were fine letting the world know that—even if the world was just our home." She sighed. "I remember wishing for mistletoe just like that after they died. I even imagined hanging it in my own home one day…with my own husband and my own little girl. I wished for that on every single birthday candle and every single coin throughout the rest of my childhood. Not an unlimited supply of candy, not a trip to the zoo, not a new teddy bear. Just a sprig of mistletoe."

"And?"

"Once I was finally old enough to have my own home, that wish had slipped my mind." Her voice turned to a whisper. "And, well, now it's too late."

For the umpteenth time since they'd met, Rory wanted to reach out, pull her into his arms and simply hold her, the need to protect her from the world overwhelming. Yet for the umpteenth time he resisted, in fear of driving her away.

They'd made progress over the past eighteen hours. Big progress. And the last thing he wanted to do was set them back by coming on too strong.

Instead, he changed the subject. "Apparently your frames are causing quite a stir. They're all Virginia and Delilah talked about this morning when I stopped by the diner for breakfast."

The protective wall he'd seen in her eyes began to slip down once again. "They told you about them?"

"I overheard them talking to a group of women when I sat down. Seems you might have a few people ready to place orders beyond the one you already have from Virginia."

Maggie's mouth gaped open. "Are you serious?"

"Absolutely." Pulling his cell phone from his back pocket, he glanced at the screen. "Wow, it's getting late. We better head out."

"Where are we going?"

"I said no more hints, remember?" He met her smile with one of his own. "Now grab your coat. Something warm, okay? It's looking like it could snow at any time."

"You can be a little bossy sometimes, you know that?" she teased before disappearing into her room and returning in a soft blue winter jacket and matching hat. "Luckily for me, my coat is blue. That way my lips will match by the time we get wherever you're taking me."

He looked at her mouth and swallowed, his mind

searching for a safe answer. One that wouldn't get him kicked out on his ear. "I'll do my best to keep you warm."

SHE POINTED OUT THE passenger-side window as Rory drove the back road skirting the shores of Lake Shire. "Do you see that little inlet? My uncle used to launch our rowboat from that very spot."

"Did you help row?"

"I tried, though I doubt I was much help. A little girl doesn't have all that much power."

He slid a glance at her. "I bet Doug didn't mind."

Maggie couldn't help but smile. "He didn't. He was— and is—the most patient man I've ever known. Except for…you."

"You think I'm patient?"

"How could I not? You've put up with my grumpy face since the first moment we met. And you're still here." Feeling suddenly foolish, she concentrated on the view of the lake, pulling herself back to safer waters. "One time I came for a visit and we stayed out in my uncle's boat all day. We ate, we fished and we read books right there in the middle of the lake."

"He helped you, didn't he?" Rory asked as he slowed for a stoplight.

"More than I can ever say."

"Any chance he'll make it back from Europe in time for Christmas?"

She shrugged. "He's going to try. But I'm not sure I'm ready."

Rory turned right and then left, the view of the lake

now obstructed by trees and occasional homes and businesses. "Ready? For what?"

"I want to be in a better place when he comes. I want to have taken some of the steps I promised I would take."

"And what, exactly, did you tell him you'd do?" Rory slowed as the truck moved from asphalt onto cobblestone, the bumpy feel beneath the tires taking her by surprise.

"That I'd find the strength he seems to think I have." She glanced at the historic brick buildings and whimsical storefronts that lined both sides of the unfamiliar street. "What is this?"

He pulled into a parking spot in front of a gourmet pet store, a mischievous smile lighting his face. "This is Lake Shire Square. When you were a kid, this was just a run-down section of the downtown area that everyone avoided. Until about five years ago that is, when your uncle spearheaded a committee to oversee some much-needed changes. And—" he gestured toward the windshield "—voilà!"

"I don't know what to say. I had no idea Uncle Doug was involved in something like this."

Grabbing hold of the door handle on his side of the truck, Rory winked in her direction. "So? Are you ready?"

"For what?"

"I want to show you something."

"And I don't suppose you're going to tell me what that something is?"

"You suppose right." With a laugh, he hopped out of the truck.

Giving up, she zipped her jacket to the top and stepped out, finding Rory's hand on her arm before she'd even reached the walkway. "Did you work for the government at some point? FBI? CIA?"

"Nope." He dropped back a step and guided her around a patch of ice, still grasping her arm. "Some surprises can be good, you know."

"Maybe for someone else they can be," she said, regretting the words as soon as she'd said them. Today was about having fun. And fun she was determined to have. She owed Rory that much.

Shaking her head free of the thoughts that threatened to zap her energy and send her running for home, she forced herself to focus on the various shops they passed on their way to their mystery destination. There was a bakery, a café, a salon, an antiques shop, an upscale clothing store, a gently used children's resale shop and—

"Oooh, Rory, look." She stopped under the shingled sign for Lake Shire Gifts & Things and pointed toward the window display. It didn't take long to see that the shop had a very upscale, almost untouchable feel to its inventory, a fact that surprised her. In a town like Lake Shire, where so many people opted to live because of the rustic surroundings, items like china statues and glass sculptures didn't really fit. Vacationers to the area weren't likely to go home with those kinds of items, either.

Rory tugged the door open and gestured her inside the shop, an unreadable expression an his face.

"We don't have to go in now. Not if it's going to make us late for wherever it is we're going."

"We're here."

She stopped halfway through the door. "We're here?"

Before he could answer, a woman in her mid-fifties approached them. "Mr. O'Brien, I assume?"

Maggie glanced back at Rory, watched him extend his hand toward the woman. "Yes. And you must be Ms. Johansen?"

"Please. Call me Iris." The woman's blue-gray eyes turned in her direction. "And you must be Maggie, yes?"

She nodded automatically, Iris's warm hand on hers doing little to ease the confusion she knew was furrowing her brow.

"Feel free to look around. As you can see, the show-room space is ample for a shop like this." Iris motioned toward a door at the far side of the room. "There's also a small office in back, as well as a room that I use for unpacking items when they come in. Right now it's fur-nished with a series of shelving units—all of which I could leave behind if that would be helpful."

"Thank you, Iris," Rory said. "Maggie, shall we?"

"Shall we what?" she whispered as the shop owner headed back to her post behind the register. "Rory, what's going on? Why are we here?"

"To see what you think."

Maggie looked around at the various shelves and the breakable items they held. "It's nice but—" looking toward the counter, she lowered her voice still further

"—it doesn't really invite leisurely browsing. Not the kind that lulls people into buying, anyway."

"What do you mean?"

"Well, for starters, there's the merchandise. It's more suitable to city people."

He leaned against a nearby wall. "How so?"

"Take these statues. Do they really seem like the kind of things people are going to use to decorate their second homes? Or the kind of souvenirs people would want to buy to remember their vacation to Lake Shire?" Lifting a china figure, she continued. "A wooden rowboat or a plaque about fishing would sell better. At least in a town like this.

"And…and where are the postcards for the vacationers? And the cutesy refrigerator magnets that people can bring home when their trip is over?" she asked, as much to herself as Rory.

"And what about the hand-decorated picture frames for displaying their favorite vacation pictures?" he offered. "Or the one-of-a-kind Christmas ornaments for decorating their trees?"

"Exactly." She set the figurine down, Rory's words registering in her mind. "Whoa. Wait a minute. What's going on here? What, exactly, are you up to, mister?"

He folded his arms across his muscled chest, visible through the opening of his leather jacket. "Iris is moving."

Maggie stared at him, waiting for further clarification.

When none came, she stepped closer. "What does her moving have to do with me?"

"She's looking to lease this place."

"She's looking to lease this…" The words trailed from Maggie's mouth as reality dawned. "Wait. You think I should rent it?"

"It's a dream, isn't it?"

She swallowed over the lump that sprang up in her throat.

Was it? Was it really her dream to run a gift shop of her own?

It has been for years….

"I…"

Dropping his hands to his sides, Rory stepped close, his gaze pinning hers with a fire she couldn't ignore. "Think about it, Maggie. This is the perfect place. The perfect setting to sell the kinds of things you make— things you just said would be a better fit for a place like Lake Shire."

"But that was before." She glanced around the room once again. "Before I knew why you were showing it to me. When I thought it was just a…just a—" She stopped, unsure of how best to finish her thought.

"When you thought it was just a regular store with no connection to you and your dreams."

"It is."

He took hold of her upper arms gently, his eyes pleading with hers. "But it doesn't have to be, Maggie. Don't you see that? You have talent. I could see that right away. And it's not just me, Maggie. Delilah and Virginia saw it with your frame. You're good. Really good. So why not give it a whirl? See how it goes?"

Was Rory right? Could she really make something like this work?

"I don't know, Rory. I just don't know."

He dropped his hand to the small of her back, guiding her forward. "Let's just look at the rest of the place. After all, it doesn't hurt to imagine, does it?"

He was right. It didn't.

Slowly but surely, they made their way through the rest of the store. "This must be the office Iris mentioned," he said, pointing toward an open doorway.

"Hmm." Maggie peeked into the tiny room, which was just large enough to house a desk, but had a small window overlooking the trendy café next door. "It *is* an appealing location."

"And this is where she unpacks her items…."

Maggie followed him back out of the office, only to stop in her tracks. "Oh, Rory, this is perfect!"

"What? You like the shelves?"

Shaking her head, she rushed to explain. "No. The space." She walked into the center of the room and spun around. "If you got rid of the shelves, there'd be room for a worktable. A big one. Perfect for painting and gluing and whatever else I'm working on at the time."

A smile tugged at his lips. "You're right. It would make a perfect workroom."

A workroom. For making her frames…and her ornaments…and her wall decorations…and—

"Oh, Rory, I just don't know. I mean, it's something I used to think about. But to actually *do* it?"

"I think you'd be a hit around here."

She glanced up at him to find the heartfelt belief he

had in her etched across every inch of his face. It was almost more than she could take at that moment. "There's so much to think about. I wasn't planning on staying in Lake Shire. This was just supposed to be a place to—" She stopped, unable to produce the words.

"To get back on your feet?" he offered, his husky tone making her look at him closely. Rory O'Brien, with his heart-stopping smile and kindhearted ways, believed in her. Truly believed in her. Why, she didn't know, but he did.

She nodded.

"Reaching for one of your dreams sounds like a mighty good way to do that, don't you think?"

Chapter Fourteen

It was almost too much to take in at one time. She'd come to Lake Shire for a change—a place to start doing all the basics she'd neglected, like eating and sleeping. And now, less than a week later, she was actually contemplating plans for a future.

Her future.

Maggie stopped just outside her door and turned, her breath catching at the sight of the man not more than two steps behind. As well as being handsome and charming and fun to spend time with, Rory was the kind of man that made her believe.

In second chances…

In dreams…

And in herself.

"You've got a lot to think about. And I suppose I better do something to earn that paycheck your uncle keeps sending me every two weeks." He clasped his hands in front of his mouth and blew, the angry pink of his skin a reminder he'd left his gloves in the truck. "But if you want to talk or to bounce ideas around, you know where to find me. I like that kind of stuff. It's fun, you know?

Reaching out, she took hold of his hands, rubbed them gently. "So your hint—about Jeannie? You meant the kind that grants wishes, didn't you?"

A sly smile crept across his face. "You found me out."

She tilted her head to the side and studied the way the hallway light seemed to pick out both dark and pale hues in his ocean-blue eyes. "Can I ask you a question?"

"Shoot."

"Why do my wishes mean so much to you?"

For a moment she didn't think he was going to respond. But finally he did, the words coming hesitantly as he looked into her eyes. "Because *you* do."

She closed her eyes momentarily as his hands touched her face, the feel of his skin against hers setting off a slew of emotions she wasn't ready to analyze. Not yet, anyway.

"Maggie, I can't stop thinking about you—"

Rising up on tiptoe, she stopped him with a kiss. "Go on. Get back to work."

A soft groan rumbled from his lips, tickling hers in the process. "I think this is the first time in months the notion of work has been utterly distasteful."

She stepped back. "I'm sorry."

He raised her hand to his mouth. "Don't be." And with that, he was gone, disappearing down the center hallway of Lake Shire Inn, his happy whistle trailing behind.

Blowing a wisp of hair from her forehead, Maggie inserted the key into the lock and turned it, a faint aroma of paint beckoning her inside and reminding her of the decision she had to make.

There was so much to take in. So much to consider.

Could she really do it? Could she really run her own gift shop—making virtually all of the items herself?

She glanced toward the heart-shaped ornament she'd made the night before. It was good. She knew that. Any hesitation she might have had about that had been wiped away by Rory's positive words.

With careful fingers, she lifted the ornament off the table and carried it toward the tree. If she hung it on a branch to the left, the light shining in from the window would make the silver inscription leap out.

Perhaps a small shelf light would create the same effect in the shop?

The thought caught her up short. Unsure of what to think or do, she shifted, trying to get a better look at her uncle's gift. As it did with the hand-painted heart, the light streaming in from the window made the wishing ball sparkle.

"Wishes," she whispered. "Wishes…"

She'd wished for a knitting lesson and Rory had made it happen.

She'd wished to find new ways to remember her family and Rory had made it happen.

She'd wished for her own gift shop and Rory had put her on track to make it happen.

If Maggie did this, it would change everything. She would have a reason to get up each morning…an excuse to craft the hours away…a reason to stay in Lake Shire, closer to her uncle…

And Rory.

IT FELT GOOD TO STRETCH out his legs, to walk a distance greater than the two or three feet he'd crossed from ladder to wall and back again all afternoon. Sure, he'd made good progress on the corner room, but still…

He stopped outside Maggie's door, thoughts of a late-night skating excursion tugging his mouth into a smile. It would be good for both of them. He needed the exercise; she needed the fresh air and an opportunity to laugh. And then maybe, over a hot chocolate, they could talk more about her shop.

Buying that store was the ticket. Of that he was sure.

Since they'd met, the only thing that had put a lasting smile on her face and hope in her eyes was her crafts. If Maggie could surround herself with that every day, maybe she'd begin to heal.

Really heal.

His mind made up, he knocked, the sound of his fist echoing through the empty hallway.

Nothing.

He stepped back. A shaft of light from beneath the door created a shadow of his boots on the wood-planked floor. Perhaps she was busy working on a frame or another ornament? He held his ear to the door and listened.

Again, there was nothing. Maybe she'd gone to dinner?

Disappointment weighed down his tired shoulders and propelled him toward the picture window at the end of the hallway. He knew he should be glad she'd left her room. It was, after all, progress. But the thought of spending the evening with her—skating, hanging out, dreaming—had been more than a little appealing.

He looked down into the parking lot and noted the two lone cars.

His hunter-green pickup truck. And her little white Taurus.

Confused, he retraced his steps to her door and knocked again, this time straining to make out any semblance of life on the other side. And that's when he heard it.

Maggie was crying.

Not the gut-wrenching sobs that had torn at his heart just the other day. No, these were much more muted. As if she'd been crying for hours.

He knocked again. "Maggie, it's Rory. Are you okay?"

There was no answer.

"I'm not going to let myself in this time. But if you need something…if you need anything…I'm here."

He leaned his forehead against the door as the muted cries continued, his words, his offer, having no discernible impact whatsoever.

Chapter Fifteen

He was later than he'd intended, but tracking down a sprig of mistletoe wasn't as easy as he'd imagined. Lake Shire's lone Christmas shop had only plastic versions—an unacceptable choice when trying to fulfill a childhood dream.

Fortunately for Rory, the shop owner had recommended a florist on the edge of town. The location, however, had entailed a long drive.

It wasn't that he had to punch a clock at the inn, because he didn't. Doug didn't care if Rory worked during the day or the night, as long as he got the work done. But he'd hoped to catch Maggie early enough to talk her into having breakfast with him. Showing up at her door at nearly eleven o'clock made breakfast a little tough.

He tucked the mistletoe under his left arm while he held tight to the bag of penny candy he'd purchased at Russ's shop downtown. Not knowing exactly what kind of candy she liked, Rory had taken a little from every barrel in the store. This way, he was sure to cover both wishes at one time—even if her childhood wish for an unlimited supply of candy had been pushed out of first place by the sight of her parents kissing under the mistletoe.

Who said she had to choose one over the other?

A wish was a wish, after all, wasn't it?

"Maggie? You home?" He knew it was a stupid question. Her car was in the parking lot, just as it had been the night before. Same spot. Same turn to the wheel. He leaned forward, pressed his ear to the door and listened.

Nothing.

"Maggie…I have something for you. Two things, actually." But even as the words left his mouth he knew she wasn't going to answer. He could feel it.

Why, though, was what he didn't get. She'd been fine yesterday—happy, even. Her eyes had absolutely lit up at the notion of running her own gift shop. He'd have had to be blind not to see it.

So why wasn't she answering the door?

You know why. Depression does that. It did it to Reardon, too.

Reardon.

Rory had to do something. He couldn't sit by and watch someone as beautiful and talented as Maggie slip into a hole by herself.

No. He had to get her out. Even if it was someone else's arms that actually did the pulling.

SHE ROLLED OVER AND stared at the wall, willing herself to block out his knocking. When was he going to get it? When was he going to realize she didn't want to see him?

He'd been persistent the night before, his footsteps finally retreating after a solid twenty minutes. This morning's visit had been closer to ten, but still…

And now here he was again.

There was a part of her that wanted to fling open the door and beg him to leave her alone. That, at least, would stop the knocking.

But the other part—the part that was more tired than she'd ever been—simply didn't have the energy to get off the bed and walk into the living room. And besides, he was a nice guy. Just because she had some sort of curse around her didn't mean she had to get nasty.

He'd get the point. Eventually.

"Maggie? It's Delilah. Are you okay?"

She rose up on one elbow, her eyes heavy from shed tears. Did she dare open the door? Dare take the chance that somehow she could make Delilah—and thereby Rory—understand?

It was worth a try.

A third knock sounded. "Please, Maggie. I'd really like to talk with you."

She slipped out of bed and padded across the living-room floor, the pitter-patter of her feet in stark contrast to the insistent knocking that guided her steps. When she reached the door, she opened it a crack to find Delilah's concerned face looming there.

"Maggie!"

She glanced down at the floor, only to find two brightly colored gift bags filled with tissue paper mere inches from the woman's feet. "What's that?" Maggie whispered.

"That? That's a few gifts from a man who's more than a little worried about you."

Tears welled in her eyes at the reproach in Delilah's voice. "I'm sorry. I really am. But I can't let this thing between us continue."

Delilah gestured past her. "May I come in?"

"Of course." She backed up and watched as Delilah moved across the room, only to stop when her boot met something on the floor. Something round and silver...

The wishing ball.

Maggie swallowed. "I'm sorry. I—"

The woman bent down and retrieved the gleaming ornament. "Oh, Maggie, this is beautiful." Without waiting for a response, Delilah marched across the room and hung it on the tree, her branch selection a near-perfect match to the one it had graced less than twelve hours earlier. Before Maggie's tirade had caused it to go skittering across the floor.

"It was from my uncle. Seems he's just as determined as Rory to push me forward. Only there are limits to what forward can and can't be."

Delilah turned, sorrow etching creases beside her eyes. "Can we sit for a few minutes?"

Maggie shrugged.

The woman crossed to the sofa and sat down. "Come. Sit."

She did as she was told.

"You're struggling, aren't you?"

And like a dam bursting, the tears began to flow. Maggie felt Delilah's arms pulling her close as the tears turned into sobs and her shoulders began to shake uncontrollably.

Seconds flowed into minutes and minutes into longer, but still Delilah held her. There was no hurrying. No attempt to hush the sounds with empty words. And for that, Maggie was grateful.

Finally, she was able to catch her breath. "I'm sorry, Delilah. I didn't mean to go on like that. Really, I'm doing better. I'm trying, anyway."

The woman peered at her closely. "Go on like what? You're hurting. You've been through a lot in your relatively short life."

"Sometimes I'm afraid I'm never going to stop crying."

"But you do. And it's in those moments that you take your steps." Delilah pushed a strand of hair behind Maggie's ear.

She nodded. "Those steps can only go so far, though."

"Why?"

"Because I don't want to hurt like I have this past year ever again."

"I'm sorry, Maggie, but I don't understand."

Pulling her feet onto the sofa, she wrapped her arms around her legs. "When my parents died, I was devastated. One minute I was a normal, happy kid and the next…I was an orphan, taken in by a well-meaning aunt who did her best. But it wasn't *my* family—mine was ripped from my world in the blink of an eye."

Delilah touched Maggie's knee and gave a gentle squeeze. "Ahhh, and then, when you finally had your own family…you lost them, as well."

She turned to look at her. "I couldn't survive that a third time."

"Those two incidents were unrelated, Maggie. You have to know that."

Dropping her feet back to the ground, she stood and made her way to the window, which overlooked one of the five fingers of Lake Shire. "But don't you see? They *were* related."

"How? They happened more than twenty years apart."

Maggie lifted her hand to shield her eyes from the weak winter sunlight shimmering atop the water. "They both had *me* in common."

Delilah sucked in her breath. "You?"

"Those were my parents…and my husband and child."

In a second Delilah was beside her at the window, her gently lined hand grabbing hold of Maggie's upper arm. "And they were accidents, hon. Unfortunate, tragic, *unrelated* accidents."

"My heart was broken as a result, both times. I won't put myself in a position to have it happen a third time. I can't." Placing her hand on top of Delilah's, she gave a gentle squeeze. "My heart can't take this kind of hurt ever again."

"So then you *do* have feelings for Rory?"

Maggie turned back to the window, inhaling the courage she needed to say the words that had to be said. "It doesn't matter whether I do or not. All that matters is I can't."

"Can't or won't?"

"Does it really matter?" She pointed toward the water. "When I was a little girl, I used to sit out on that lake and wish for a second chance at love. A grown-up kind of love that I naively thought would be forever. Eventually, when the time was right, I got that second chance. Only it didn't last forever. It, too, got ripped away. And the hurt was a million times worse the second time around. In fact, if I could, I'd go with them. Now."

"Don't say that!"

"But it's true."

"Did you wish you were dead when you were making those frames the other day? Or when Virginia was falling all over herself wanting to hire you to make one for her?"

"No. Not at that moment."

"Did you wish you were dead when you were walking through the gift shop in the village, envisioning what it might be like if it were yours?"

"No. But I...wait. How do you know about that?"

"Rory told me."

"Rory," she repeated softly. "Somehow that man has elbowed his way into whatever part of my heart remains intact."

"But don't you see? That's a good thing."

"Not if something happens to him, as seems to be the case with everyone I touch."

"So you're willing to let another chance slip through your fingers based on a what-if?"

"If it means keeping Rory safe...yes."

Horror chased confusion from Delilah's eyes. "Tell me

you don't believe your loved ones were cursed because of you."

Maggie shrugged. "How can I not?"

"Because that's not the way life works." Gentle arms enveloped her in a hug. "Aren't you glad you had those early years with your parents?"

"Of course. I wouldn't trade them for anything."

"And the time with your husband and daughter?"

"The same."

"Then why would you cheat yourself out of time with another wonderful person? They're what make life worth living." Delilah's arms loosened their grip and Maggie stepped back. "He cares about you, Maggie. He really does."

"I know." And she did. "He's been so kind and so supportive and…"

"And what?"

She stared at the floor, unsure of what to say and how to say it. Finally, she simply shrugged.

"Let him be all those things. It's a wonderful gift to have someone in your corner. It truly is. And he believes in you, Maggie. If he didn't, he never would have shown you that shop yesterday."

Delilah was right.

"The day I brought you your frame, he'd shown up on my doorstep with a box of craft supplies. Said he found it in one of the empty rooms at the inn."

A corner of Delilah's mouth twitched.

"Oh, trust me…I know he didn't find it. But that's what got me going again. That's what got me—"

"Hoping again?"

Maggie tried the woman's words on for size, even though she knew they were the perfect fit. But the delay gave her time—time to get a handle on the tears that threatened to spill down her cheeks for what had to be the hundredth time that day. "Hoping that maybe I can have another chance."

"Then don't set boundaries before you see where it can take you."

Chapter Sixteen

She peered at her reflection in the mirror, finding that the hint of hope, as well as her plans for the evening, had brought an unfamiliar shine to her eyes. A shine that was more than a little welcome.

For hours after Delilah left, Maggie had sat at the kitchen table making lists—items she felt would do well in the shop, steps she needed to take to market the store, custom-order work she could offer to increase her appeal. The fact that she talked through some of her thoughts using things she'd learned from Jack only served as proof of his lasting place in her heart.

The baby items she'd allowed herself to consider had been a bit more difficult, but even with that she'd found a way to honor her daughter. Everlasting Smiles would be a line of custom-order frames created for the sole purpose of marking various milestones in a child's life—First Step, First Smile, First Birthday, etc. Each frame would have a tiny leaf emblem on the back as a reminder of Natalie's first smile.

It was as if Delilah's visit had unlocked a door in Maggie's heart, giving her access to a place where there were no walls between the past and the present, and where the future could coexist with both of them.

Her future.

Inhaling courage into her lungs, Maggie rummaged through her purse until she found the directions she'd used less than a week earlier. She knew there was no guarantee Rory would be home, but it was a chance she was willing to take. She owed him that much.

She stepped into the hall, stopping to retrieve the packages she and Delilah had left outside the door. The least Maggie could do was give him the opportunity to hand them to her as he'd intended.

After she apologized. And after she said thank-you.

The drive to Rory's house was shorter than she re-membered, despite the frequent stops she made to grab real-estate flyers along the way. A few of the places she checked out were mother-in-law quarters. Although not her ideal, it was certainly an option to consider, at least until Maggie knew whether her shop would succeed.

Her shop.

It was hard to believe she'd been in Lake Shire less than a week. She'd arrived at her uncle's inn with a heart so heavy it threatened to stop beating. Yet now, it was lighter somehow.

She made the final turn onto Rory's street, finding his house easy to pick out thanks to the colorful lights from the Christmas tree that graced his front room. Slipping the car into Park, she turned off the engine and sat star-ing up at the place.

There was so much she wanted to say to him. So many

ideas about the shop she wanted to share. But there was a part of her that was afraid, too.

For days he'd gone out of his way to be nice. And when she hadn't been actively pushing him away, she'd been holding him at arm's length.

Except when they kissed.

She closed her eyes at the memory of his lips on hers, her heart rate accelerating on cue. She hadn't dreamed of anything like that when she came to Lake Shire. And wasn't sure she'd ever want it again.

But it had been special nonetheless.

Because *he* was special.

Rory O'Brien was the kind of person who made you feel good. His positive outlook, encouraging spirit and thoughtful ways were rare gifts. And he had them all. The fact that he wanted to share them with her was nothing short of a blessing.

She stepped from the car armed with the bags he'd left and a little something extra she'd tucked inside her purse. Slowly, she made her way up to the door, her determination to do the right thing overshadowed by a fear that seemed to grow with each step she took.

What if he was angry? What if he slammed the door and told her to go home? What if he simply didn't answer?

"He cares about you, Maggie. He really does."

With any luck, Delilah was right. Just as she seemed to be about everything else…

Maggie knocked, and the footsteps she heard brought a smile to her lips that only grew wider when they came face-to-face.

"Maggie?"

"Hi. I hope you don't mind that I just stopped by." She lifted the items he'd left. "But it looks as if you wanted to give me something."

A dimple appeared in first one cheek and then the other. "And you—Little Miss I Don't Like Surprises— didn't peek?"

"Nope. So I figured I'd bring them over here along with something else."

"Something else?" he asked.

A squadron of butterflies took flight in her stomach the moment he cocked his head to study her. She gulped. "Yes."

"Do you plan on cluing me in?"

She considered making him wait, stringing him along the way he had done to her about the shop. But in the end she relented, her mouth desperate to do something other than find his. "I brought an apology."

"You don't owe me any apologies."

"I don't agree." A gust of wind kicked up and skittered across the front porch, making her teeth chatter. "I—I was w-wrong—"

He reached for her and tugged her inside, closing the door against the cold. "If you insist on apologizing, I insist you come inside. Your uncle will have my hide if you get sick standing on my front porch."

She couldn't help but laugh. Partially because Rory had such a sweet way of putting things and partially because she knew he was right.

"Can I take your coat?" he asked as he took the packages from her hands and set them on a hall table.

Nodding, she allowed him to slip it off her shoulders. "I don't want to barge in on your night, so I won't stay long. I just—"

"Barge in on my night? Are you kidding?" He hung her coat on a hook beside the door and then turned to face her. "Your being here *makes* my night."

She felt her face warm at his words. "I just wanted to apologize for ignoring your knock last night and again this morning. It's just that…well, I was in a bad place and I didn't know how to get out."

For a moment he said nothing, his gaze playing across her face before skimming slowly down her body, the gesture making her glad she'd taken the time to put on a nice pair of black corduroy pants and a white V-neck sweater. The boots had been an afterthought, one he seemed to like based on the appreciative double take they earned. When his visual inventory was done, he offered a smile that nearly melted her knees. "You're here now. That's all that matters."

"No, it's not," she protested. "You've been so nice to me since the beginning. You've listened to me. You've encouraged me. You've done so many sweet things. All of which leads me to the second reason for my visit."

He brought his hand to the small of her back and guided her toward the hearth room. "Don't say another word. Not until you come in and sit down."

She did as she was told, sinking onto the couch beside his muscular frame. When she'd caught her breath, she continued, though his sheer presence made it hard to focus on anything besides him. "I wanted to say thank-you. Everything you've done for me so far has been above and beyond, but the box of craft supplies? Well, that was my puff of air."

"Puff of air?"

"To get my wings up off the floor," she explained, her voice growing quiet as she pondered the enormity of what she was saying—what she hoped to get across. "I've been so lost, Rory. Simply moving through a life I no longer wanted."

He grimaced at her words. "Please don't say that."

She brought the tips of her fingers to his lips even as she tried not to remember the way they'd felt against her own. "I still hurt at their loss. And I always will. But making a future for myself doesn't mean they disappear."

The words were so much like the ones Delilah had spoken during their knitting lesson, words that had been hard to take in, yet were everything Maggie needed to hear. She was here because it wasn't her time.

"That shop you showed me? I want to give it a go. I want to chase that dream…see where it leads." She felt him studying her closely, yet she didn't mind. "It's something I considered a long time ago before I had another—far more important—purpose to my days. Now that that purpose is no longer there—" her voice faltered "—I need to find something else to keep my feet moving. Something that will get me through life until I see them again. I think the shop will do that."

His brow furrowed momentarily, a frown soon pushed away by a slow, thoughtful smile. "The supplies did that?"

"*You* did that." Her breath hitched when she felt his

hand on her face, his thumb wiping away a lone tear. "You keep granting me these wishes I didn't even realize I had. And they're changing me...they're giving me—" She stopped, closed her eyes as his hand caressed her jaw.

"They're giving you what?"

"Hope," she whispered.

When he didn't respond, she opened her eyes, saw him studying her with a look she couldn't identify. "What?"

"Wishes have a way of doing that, you know."

"Do they now?" she teased.

"I happen to know you have a few more out there."

"I do?"

Nodding, he stood and ventured into the hallway, returning with the two bags she'd brought over. He set the first one in her lap. "Open this first."

She looked from the bag to him and back again. "What did you do?"

"I listened."

"You're good at that." She pulled the handles of the gift bag apart and peeked inside. The assortment of her favorite penny candies caught her by surprise. "Candy?"

"It's not exactly the lifetime supply you mentioned, but it'll keep you busy for a while." He dropped onto the sofa beside her. "The chocolate caramel twists were some of my favorites growing up."

She looked at him through the misty haze that suddenly filled her eyes. "How do you do it? How do you remember all of this?"

He shrugged, then pulled his hand out from behind his back to reveal the second bag. "Now open this one."

"Rory, I can't. You've done too much already."

He set it on her lap. "Please. This one is special."

"They've all been special." And she meant it. She pried the handles of the second bag apart, a familiar scent wafting through the opening as she did so. "Oh, my gosh…you didn't."

Reaching into the bag, she retrieved the tissue-wrapped plant from inside, the mist in her eyes finding its way down her cheeks.

"There's no reason you can't hang it in your uncle's suite. It's a memory, you know?"

"A wonderful memory," she whispered. Raising it above his head, she leaned in for a kiss, only to stop just short of his lips. "Thank you, Rory. Thank you for everything."

HE CUPPED THE BACK OF HER head with his hand and pulled her close, the feel of her mouth on his obliterating any restraint he had left. When her lips parted ever so slightly, he pressed on, his tongue mingling with hers as his hands dropped to her waist.

His body hardened as she scooted closer, slipping her arms around his neck. Dropping his lips to her chin and then her neck, he found himself wishing it was summer. A camisole or halter top would give easier access to the skin he longed to touch, to memorize.

"Maggie," he groaned as she wiggled closer, the swell of her breasts visible through her V-neck as she pressed against him. "You have no idea how often I think about you. You're on my mind all the time."

She put her hand against his chest and leaned back. "Why?"

It was a question he couldn't believe she could ask, when the answers seemed so obvious. "Because you're sweet. You're special. You're..." He pulled her onto his lap and nuzzled the side of her face with his nose. "You drive me wild."

"Wild?" she echoed, the word morphing into a soft moan as his hands traveled to the bottom of her sweater and slipped beneath the hemline.

"Absolutely, positively wild." Slowly, he moved his hands upward, savored the feel of her soft skin beneath his palms, the sensation broken only by the silky bra that blocked his path. Daunted for only a second, he unhooked the clasps, felt the material give way against the push of her rounded breasts.

He stopped, met her eyes with his own, wordlessly pleaded for permission to continue. She, too, spoke without words as she grabbed hold of her sweater and lifted it over her head.

SHE WATCHED HIM FROM beneath her lashes, his moan of appreciation giving her the courage to continue. If he noticed the angry scars on her arm, he didn't mention them. Instead he simply stared at her in awe.

"God, you are beautiful, Maggie," he murmured as he jumped to his feet and clasped her hands in his. "Absolutely beautiful." He leaned in and whispered against her ear, "Are you sure? I mean really, really sure?"

She nodded, savoring the sensation of his breath on her skin. "I'm sure."

"Then let's go upstairs," he said, his voice husky with desire. "I want this to be perfect."

"It *is* perfect…right here." She tipped her head toward the twinkling lights of the Christmas tree, the nibble of his lips on her neck making her body tingle. "It's magical."

"Being here with you is what makes it magical." His lips dropped lower, trailing his hands as they moved from her shoulders to her breasts. With quiet urgency he teased each nipple with his tongue, arousing her more.

When he stopped to look at her, she reached for the buttons of his shirt and slowly undid each one, the feel of the cloth beneath her fingertips more than a little exciting. As she neared the bottom, the maroon-colored fabric fell open, affording an unobstructed view of his muscular chest….

She wanted him. And he, no doubt, wanted her. She could see it in his eyes every bit as much as she could feel it in his touch.

They made their way over to the tree, where he knelt on the rug and pulled her to him. Slowly, deliberately, he unfastened the buttons on her jeans, slid them down her thighs until they pooled at her feet. Then, reaching up, he inched her black lace panties down, a look of sheer admiration on his face.

For the past week this man had listened to her thoughts, remembered her wishes. And one by one he'd made them come true, changing her life in the process.

Now it was *her* turn.

Maggie took charge, unfastening first his belt and then the button that held his jeans closed. Boldly she took the zipper between her teeth and lowered it, the most intimate parts of her growing wet with desire at the sight of his body craning toward hers.

He pulled her to him, his hands resuming their exploration. Every caress, every kiss, every nibble, every stroke drove her closer and closer to the edge.

She met his lips with her own, then moved lower—to his shoulders, his chest, his stomach, the inside of his thighs… When she took him in her mouth he cried out with desire, tangling his strong fingers in her hair.

After several long moments he coaxed her back up, only to shift both of them to the floor. Covering her body with his, he entered her with a gentle authority that left her spinning. She moaned with pleasure at the feel of his length inside her, the rhythmic motions making it nearly impossible to breathe as he rose and fell against her again and again, their release coming at the same heart-stopping moment.

FOR HOURS HE SIMPLY HELD her as she slept, his eyes commanding every inch of her body and every nuance of her face to his memory. It didn't matter that he had to work in a few short hours, or that he hadn't gotten so much as a wink of sleep yet. The only thing Rory cared about was lying in his arms. Sleeping peacefully.

Maggie was everything he'd ever wanted. She was sweet, yet sexy. Funny, yet serious. Smart, yet innocent. And for whatever reason, she seemed to care about him, too.

She'd been through so much. The angry red scar on her forearm was visual proof of that, while the push-pull of the past week signaled the part he couldn't see.

But that was about to change.

He was going to keep her safe from here on out, loving her with everything he had. And he was going to give her the life she deserved—one filled with realized dreams and answered wishes.

His mind made up, he finally closed his eyes, the sweet scent that was Maggie filling his senses as he drifted off to sleep.

Chapter Seventeen

Maggie rolled onto her side and nestled her head into the pillow, a shaft of sunlight warming the left side of her face as she became aware of a vaguely pleasant smell.

Mmm, bacon.

"Bacon?" Pushing up onto her elbow, she looked around at the sofa, the rug, the coffee table, Rory's Christmas tree...

Rory's Christmas tree?

"How on earth..." Confusion overtook her as she peered down at the unfamiliar blanket she clutched to her chest. Slowly, she pulled it back, and felt guilt sweeping in. "Oh no...oh no...what have I done?"

A door on the far side of the room opened. "Maggie? Are you awake?"

Rory. She'd been with Rory last night. They'd made love....

Suddenly she remembered it all. Every touch. Every kiss. Every thrust of desire. Every moan of pleasure.

"Stop right there," she begged, using the blanket as a shield. "Please. I—I have to get dressed. I have to go home."

"There's no rush, sweetheart. I'm making breakfast right now."

She pushed herself to her feet, her heart thumping wildly. "I have to leave. *Now.*"

He came around the sofa, opening his arms as he did. She backed up into the branches of the tree. "No. Please. I—I can't. Oh…I can't. Not again."

His smile faltered. "Maggie, what's wrong?"

"I made an awful mistake," she said in a tear-choked voice. "An awful, awful mistake."

"What are you talking…" And then he stopped, her words wiping every last glimmer of joy from his face. "Maggie…please. Don't say that. You were happy last night. *I* was happy."

"I wasn't thinking," she protested over the tears.

"You're right, you weren't." He reached for her. "You were *feeling,* Maggie."

"I don't want to feel! It leads to pain. Every single time."

"But it doesn't have to be like that." He reached for her again, only to have her back up farther against the tree. "I'm not going anywhere."

"Do you think they wanted to leave?"

"No, of course not. But that still doesn't mean—"

"Everyone I love disappears from my life. It's like I'm some sort of bad penny."

A look of horror flashed across his face. "Don't say that! Oh God, don't say that."

"It's true." She clutched the blanket still tighter. "First my parents…then Jack and Natalie. I can't do it again."

"You love your uncle, don't you?" Rory stepped back,

the hurt in his eyes a stark contrast to the calm of his voice. "He's still here. He's been here since you were a little girl."

Once Rory was far enough away, Maggie stepped forward, scooping up her neatly folded clothes from the top of the coffee table. "I'm sorry, Rory. I really am. But you mean too much to me to ever let this happen again."

IT WAS NEARLY THREE O'CLOCK before he arrived at the inn, and Maggie's car was nowhere to be found. Rory knew he should be grateful for her absence after the way she'd stomped all over his heart, yet he wasn't.

In the week he'd known her, Maggie sightings had become the high point of his day. The moments they actually spent together—at the diner, at his home, in her suite, at the gift shop, in the car—only served to underscore that fact.

And last night? Well, that had been like nothing he'd ever experienced before.

Sure, he'd been with other women over the years—attractive, intelligent women who'd enjoyed his company as much as he had theirs. But Maggie was different.

Her breathtaking beauty was only an exterior view of a woman who was sweet and true, honest and loyal....

Loyal.

He unlocked the front door of the inn and stepped inside, his feet leading him in a different direction than his heart begged to go. Maybe it was silly to take the hallway that bypassed Maggie's suite, but he had to. Doing otherwise would be akin to stepping in front of a moving car.

It was just as Delilah had said when he'd called her

for words of wisdom after Maggie left. He couldn't fix everything.

It was a fact that was painful to hear and even more painful to accept, but if he removed his heart from the equation he knew she was right. He'd been trying so hard to fix Maggie's pain he hadn't given her room to breathe.

The whole reason she'd come to Lake Shire was to find a way to move forward. And while he'd intended his gifts to help in that regard, they'd only served to muddy the waters.

"Some things just need time and space, Rory."

Delilah's voice filtered through his thoughts as he turned the corner into the room he was rehabbing. It made sense. It really did. But there was a part of him that was more than a little wary of that kind of advice.

He'd gone that route with Reardon and it had back-fired in ways he would regret for the rest of his life.

Could he really take that chance with Maggie?

He sat down on the pile of lumber in the center of the room and stared up at the beamed ceiling. Making love to Maggie had been everything he imagined and a million times more.

And it wasn't going to happen ever again.

The truth of the situation was like a punch to the gut, one he knew would come again and again as they ran into each other around the inn. Unfortunately, it was the way things were as long as he was working for Maggie's uncle.

Which could only mean one thing…

He needed to finish the job or find his own re-placement.

SHE WATCHED AS THE SUN slipped behind the trees, casting orange-and-red streaks across Lake Shire. So much in her life had changed since the first time she'd seen this lake.

Maggie had gone from being a lost little girl to one with hope for a second chance at the family she'd lost. She'd gone from being married and having a child of her own to realizing second chances could blow up in her face, too. And she'd gone from spending her days staring aimlessly up at the ceiling to contemplating a new path—one she couldn't help but feel excited about.

Pulling her knees onto the seat, Maggie studied the lights dancing and shimmering atop the water. There was so much she regretted—every argument she'd ever had with Jack; the times she'd put Natalie in her crib to sleep rather than holding her while she napped; not remembering the diaper bag the last time.

But if she cut herself some slack, she knew things had happened the way they were meant to happen. Couples argued, yet it didn't mean they loved each other any less. Parents put their children in cribs to sleep so they could get things done. That way cuddles could happen during the all-important awake time. And as for the diaper bag…it had happened before. To her and countless other moms.

No, a forgotten diaper bag hadn't caused the accident. Fate and a patch of ice had.

But knowing that didn't make it hurt any less. It was a pain Maggie woke with every morning, and a pain she went to sleep with every night.

Yet somehow, some way, she'd managed to find some

footholds of late, the possibility of opening a gift shop of her very own the biggest one of all. Working on the frames and the ornaments had stirred something inside her. Something real. Just as realizing a dream tended to do.

And it *had* been a dream. A big one. So why not chase it? Especially now, when she had more time than she ever wanted on her hands, and no one to spend it with? It was something to get her through the days, something to put her all into without sacrificing her heart once again.

She closed her eyes in an effort to blot out the memory of Rory's mouth on hers, his hands traveling every curve of her body, his tall lean form moving above her….

No, she had to forget. She *had* to.

Chapter Eighteen

She glanced down at the documents in her hand, the whimsical logo she'd created sprawled across the top page.

Natalie's Nook.

The name had come to her in a dream, after a long day of making frames, magnets, wall hangings and table decorations. And despite the late hour and the cloud of fatigue that hovered over her, she knew it was perfect.

If not more than a little bittersweet.

Yet as her inventory had mounted, along with her excitement over the past two weeks, something was still missing.

Such as having someone to share it with.

More than once Maggie had found herself with her hand on the doorknob and Rory in her thoughts. Yet each time she'd simply made her way back to whatever craft she was working on at that moment. Rory was busy—working morning, noon and night, if the nearly constant hammering was any indication. And seeking him out to talk about the gift shop wasn't fair. Not when he had feelings for her.

And you for him...

She sat on the edge of her bed and stared down at the documents, willed her mind to focus on the legwork she'd laid in place in order to embark on her dreams. If she could just keep focused on the shop, she'd learn to forget.

Or would she?

Making crafts still left her time to think. If she designed a picture frame to reflect the beach, she recalled vacations she'd taken with Jack. If she designed a sample frame for her Everlasting Smiles line, she imagined her daughter's sweet face. If she made a tabletop decoration, she thought of colors they might have liked or ideas they might have had. And as she finished each and every project, she longed to show it to Rory.

Shifting the papers to the bed, she stood up, distracting thoughts and feelings lending an aimless quality to her mood. What was her problem? She was doing the right thing. She really was.

She just hadn't expected to hurt so much.

RORY WAVED AT VIRGINIA and headed for his favorite table in the back, the exhaustion of his fourteen-day workathon leaving him with aches from head to toe. Throwing himself into the inn's restoration had been a good call, the long days keeping him busy. The busier he was, the less time he had to think and second-guess his every move.

Unfortunately, the moment he slipped his hammer into his belt that all changed. In a flash he'd find himself analyzing every word he'd said, every step he'd taken, every move he could have done differently.

Which was why he'd ignored the bone-numbing exhaustion that had begged him to go home for dinner. At least at Delilah's there'd be people to talk to other than the voices in his head that refused to shut up.

"Well, would you look at what the cat dragged in," Delilah said as he stepped onto the elevated back section he preferred. "Why, I thought you'd upped and moved clear to the other side of the country since the last time we spoke. That, or you defected over to Larchmont in favor of Sam's place."

"Like the latter would ever happen." Rory rolled his eyes skyward before planting a kiss on his friend's forehead. "I mean, seriously, why on earth would I give up your stew for Sam's?"

"Why indeed."

Dropping into his favorite booth, he scooted across the bench and leaned his head against the vinyl seat back. "Ahh, now that feels good. Real good."

"You look exhausted, Rory." Delilah's eyebrows furrowed and her trademark smile disappeared.

"I am exhausted. Been working fourteen-hour days the past two weeks, trying to get things done over at the inn." He lifted his feet beneath the table and stretched them across to the other bench. "I figure the sooner I get done over there, the sooner I can move on."

Her eyebrows rose further. "Move on?"

He nodded.

"Move on where?"

"Don't know. I just think maybe it's time I see what

else is out there. I've spent my whole life in this same place."

"That's what home means, Rory."

His eyes swept across the miniature tree that graced the ledge above his table, noting the miniature frames and hearts that dotted the branches. "Oh, hey, look… there's Virginia's picture…and Tyler's…and Carly's… and yours."

"It's our staff tree. Everyone had to write something on a star and hang it on the tree—a favorite quote, a personal mantra, whatever." Delilah leaned across the booth and grabbed hold of one of the hearts. "Can you guess who this one belongs to?"

He peered at the rounded writing on the wooden star. "'Who needs men?'"

Delilah nodded.

"That would have to be Virginia. Unless Maggie started working here."

Ignoring his comment, Delilah stood up straight. "I haven't hung mine yet."

"What's yours say? Eat and be merry?"

"No. Though that might be a good alternative."

"To?"

"Love heals all wounds."

He dropped his hands into his lap. "You really believe that?"

"I really do."

For a moment he said nothing, opting instead to grab hold of the paper-wrapped silverware and roll it back and forth across the table. "What happens if the wounds are simply too big?"

"You love harder."

"You love harder," he mumbled. "Okay...so what happens then if the love isn't wanted?"

"If that's truly the case, then I guess you move on." Delilah peered around the diner, then slid onto the bench beside Rory's feet. "But the key is finding out whether it's truly unwanted or simply pushed away out of fear."

He raked a hand across his face, the relaxing evening he'd craved slipping through his fingers with each sentence they exchanged. "But how can I counteract a fear I can't guarantee won't happen? I mean, there's no way I can be sure I'm not gonna get hit by a bus tomorrow. Life doesn't work that way. Just look at Reardon. If I'd known what he was going to do, I'd have stopped him. But I didn't. And so I couldn't."

A tender smile inched across Delilah's face. "Do you know how long I've been waiting to hear you say that?"

"Say what?" he mumbled.

"That you didn't know. You've always been so hard on yourself about that—how you should have known, how you should have done this, that or the other. But you couldn't have, because you *didn't* know. Reardon didn't tell you."

Leaning his head back, Rory stared up the ceiling. "Life happens. For better or worse. All you can do is live it the best way you know how."

"What happens if the best way involves sharing it with another person?"

He squinted at his friend. "It's a moot point when that other person doesn't want to share it with you."

"I see." Delilah scooted to the edge of the bench and stood. "Well, I guess it's okay to give up on a job when it gets too hard. Makes things easier that way."

"Wait." He dropped his feet to the floor and sat upright. "I'm not the one who gave up. Maggie did, remember?"

"I remember."

"Then how am I giving up?"

"By working yourself like a dog just so you don't have to feel."

"I'm not doing that. I'm working like this so I can—" He stopped short of admitting she was right. Only he was going about it in a slightly different way. He was working the way he was so he could *run*.

"Look, I can see you're tired. And the last thing I want to do is exhaust you further." Delilah put a friendly hand on his shoulder. "So what would you like to eat?"

He glanced over at the mini chalkboard propped against the napkin dispenser and read the day's specials. "How's the pot roast?"

She made a face. "You have to ask? It's superb."

"Okay. Then I'll take that." He eyed his friend as she turned toward the kitchen, the question that had been burning in his heart for the past two weeks finding its way to his lips. "Have you talked to her? Is she doing okay?"

"Don't you think you should ask her that yourself?" Delilah replied as she stopped just shy of the next booth.

"She doesn't want me around. She made that perfectly clear."

"Did she?"

Rory closed his eyes as his thoughts traveled a well-worn path back to the last morning he'd seen Maggie, her use of the word *mistake* hurting all over again. "Oh, she made it clear all right. Trust me on that."

"Well, maybe she just needs a little time."

"Time isn't going to do it," he argued. "She doesn't want this. She's too afraid of risking her heart again."

"Maybe she just needs to walk alone for a little while before she's ready to trust her hand to someone else again."

His friend's words hit hard, as the truth often did. "She *smacked* my hand away, Delilah. Again and again. She's doesn't want to walk—alone or otherwise."

Delilah nodded but said nothing, her thoughts as much a mystery to Rory as his own at that moment. She took a step toward the kitchen and then stopped again, glancing over her shoulder one last time. "She's walking *now*."

"What do you mean?"

"How about I show you instead."

"Show me?" he echoed.

"Come by next Saturday around eleven-thirty. I'll show you then." Delilah gestured toward the kitchen. "Now I better get that pot roast. You look like you could use a little pick-me-up."

Chapter Nineteen

"I wish I'd had your vision when I opened this place four years ago."

Maggie stepped away from the front window and stood beside Iris Johansen. "There's no guarantee that my ideas are going to increase traffic."

The woman picked up the First Steps baby frame Maggie had designed as an example of the Everlasting Smiles line, and held it out for her to see. "With items like this, there's no doubt in my mind. In fact, it almost makes me wish I could be part of this on a daily basis instead of simply your landlord."

"I don't want you to be just my landlord," Maggie protested. "I want to be able to call you and ask for suggestions if I mess up."

Iris set the frame back down. "I don't think you'll be needing suggestions from me, I really don't. But let's see what happens, okay?"

She smiled. "Okay."

Grabbing her purse from the counter, Iris took one last look around the store. "I've been meaning to ask how you're feeling. Any better at all?"

Maggie shrugged. "A little, I guess, but that's what you get for going craft-supply shopping during cold-and-flu season."

"I'd tell you to take it easy, but now that you're running a store those words are rather futile." Iris pulled her gloves from her coat pocket and slipped them on. "I wish you great success here, Maggie, I really do."

"Thank you, Iris." She took hold of the woman's hand and gave it a gentle squeeze. "And thank you for putting me in contact with that vendor friend of yours. He couldn't have done a better—and faster—job on the sign."

"My pleasure, dear." The woman approached the front door, then paused and turned back. "May this be the start of many wonderful ventures in your life."

"Thank y— oh!" She grabbed hold of the counter as the room began to spin.

In an instant, Iris was at her side. "Maggie, are you all right?"

Closing her eyes, she willed the wooziness to subside. And eventually, it relented. "I'm okay. Just got a little dizzy there for a moment."

"Perhaps I should stay?"

She waved off the woman's concern. "No. I'll be fine. I just think I need to make sleep a priority this evening."

"Well, if you're sure…"

"I am."

And then Iris was gone, closing the door on Lake Shire Gifts & Things for the very last time. Blinking back the sudden moisture in her eyes, Maggie glanced around the shop at the various items she'd made over the past three weeks—objects that had kept her hands busy and her mind occupied.

But the pace she'd been keeping surely hadn't helped her fight whatever stomach bug she'd picked up while out and about. For the most part the nausea was manageable, coming and going at odd times. The headache that seemed to be taking its place, though, wasn't as accommodating.

She stepped behind the counter and grabbed her large purse from the shelf underneath the register. Unzipping it quickly, she rummaged around in the hope of finding something that could take the edge off the pain. One by one she touched each item—her wallet, a tube of lip gloss, a small notepad, a few pens and—

"What on earth?"

Wrapping her fingers around the smooth round object near the bottom, she pulled it from her purse.

The wishing ball.

"How did this get in…" The words died away as the answer became clear. She'd put the ornament in her purse when she went to visit Rory that last time. It had looked so nice on his tree she'd wanted him to take it back. Only she never got around to giving it to him.

Because we made love instead.

Stuffing the ornament back into her purse, she gave up on the headache medicine in favor of focusing on anything other than Rory O'Brien. Fortunately for her, it was ten o'clock and time to open the store.

Her store.

"SO WHERE ARE YOU TAKING me?" Rory asked as he eyed Delilah from the passenger seat of her car. "And why won't you give me so much as a hint?"

A hint.

The word made him smile. He'd always prided himself on being a patient guy—the sort who took things as they happened. Yet here he was, wanting a hint about their destination, just like Maggie.

He pressed his head against the cool glass and watched the lake and trees and buildings whiz past. For weeks he'd been trying hard to forget about Maggie, to ignore her car in the lot of the inn, to ignore the pull in his heart to see her. Yet no matter how hard he worked, no matter how hard he tried to convince himself he was better off, he failed. Again and again.

And he knew the reason. He was in love with Maggie Monroe, plain and simple.

"Earth to Rory. Come in, Rory…"

"Huh?"

"You asked a question and I gave you an answer. But I'm thinking you didn't hear me, because you haven't said another word."

"I'm sorry. I guess I was…well, it doesn't matter."

"You're missing her, aren't you?"

"Every day."

It was a simple answer. It was also accurate.

"Then why don't you talk to her?"

He gave another simple answer. "It's like I told you the other night. She wants nothing to do with me."

"Maybe that'll change."

"I doubt it." He pointed out the windshield as Delilah

decreased their speed to accommodate the cobblestone road. "What are we doing here? Do you realize Christmas is only five days away?"

"Bah humbug!" She stopped to let a group of pedestrians cross from one side of the outdoor marketplace to the other, a scowl lowering her brows.

"I'm not bah humbug. Just look at this place—it's crazy."

"It's almost Christmas, Rory. People are shopping."

"I see that. Which brings me back to my original question…with a slightly different twist this time around. *Why* are we here? I don't need to shop."

Delilah drove slowly, her car inching down the road. "Let's just say we're doing a little window looking."

He studied the shops as they passed—Ray's Gourmet Dog Treats, Sally's Wash & Clip, Lake Shire Antiques, Last Page Bookstore. His confusion over why his friend had insisted on this little excursion was at an all-time high. "Don't you mean window *shopping?*"

"No. I mean window looking." She clapped her hands above the steering wheel and released a little squeal. "Oooh, rock-star parking!"

"Huh?"

Pointing at the vehicle emerging from a parking spot two car lengths in front of them, she squealed again. "I couldn't get a more perfect place if I tried."

"A rock star, eh? Don't they usually have chauffeurs?" His laugh echoed through the car, bringing a smile to his companion's face. "What? Why are you looking at me like that?"

"I haven't heard that laugh in far too long."

He knew she was right. He'd been burying himself in work the past few weeks—trying desperately to forget the woman living just down the hall. And at times, when he was completely focused on his work, he managed to hold thoughts of her at bay. But the moment he completed whatever task he'd been working on, she rushed into his mind once again.

"I'm sorry, Delilah. I really am. It's just…" he leaned his head against the seat back and drank in their immediate surroundings "…that keeping busy helps…" His words trailed off as the shingle sign across the street claimed his full attention.

"See? It's like I said the other night at the diner…she's walking again."

Rory's mouth grew dry as he noted the whimsical pink writing, the name nearly leaping off the wooden sign: **Natalie's Nook.**

"Wh-what happened to Iris's place?" he asked, even as the answer dawned on him. "Wait, she did it? Maggie really opened up a shop?"

Delilah grinned. "That she has. She's leasing from Iris."

"I—I don't know what to say."

"She's barely slept these past few weeks, trying to get things ready. Even when she wasn't feeling well she kept working."

"Maggie was sick?" He pulled his attention from the window display at Natalie's Nook and fixed it on his friend. "What was wrong?"

She shrugged. "A stomach bug, I guess. I kept telling

her to get some sleep, that she'd be able to fight it better with rest, but she kept on trudging."

"Is she okay now?"

"I suppose so. I haven't seen her the past few days." Delilah pinned him with an unwavering stare. "But we could go in now and check."

He looked back at the store, the pull to go inside almost more than he could bear. But Maggie didn't want him around. She'd made that perfectly clear. "I think we better leave."

"But—"

"Delilah, please." Taking a deep breath, he gestured down the road. "I've gotta get back. I have an inn to finish. And the sooner the better."

IT WAS NEARLY FIVE O'CLOCK before she came up for air, her first day more of a success than she could have ever imagined. All day long people had come in to welcome her, only to return to the register with item after item.

The holiday wall hangings had been a hit, the front-door reindeer and jolly-faced Santas the most popular of the bunch. The Everlasting Smiles line had generated a number of comments and nearly as many orders. Maggie had even taken a request for a picture frame that would document the moment a child had found his or her shadow. It was a notion that had both intrigued and saddened her at the same time. What she wouldn't give to have seen Natalie reach that stage.

The miniature artificial trees she'd used to display her handmade ornaments were nearly bare, all thoughts of a good night's rest virtually gone. Fortunately, she'd managed to work on a few projects in the back room during occasional lulls. Had she not, she'd be busy until it was time to open again in the morning.

Still, the persistent headache and momentary bouts of dizziness had to be addressed. How, though, she had no idea.

Put on soft music…close your eyes…and relax. Just like you did with Natalie.

Natalie.

Throughout the day people had asked her about the name of the shop, assuming at first that she was Natalie. The first time or two she'd felt a familiar lump in her throat, sensed a burning behind her eyes. Yet as the day wore on, she began to relish the question.

By naming the shop after her daughter, she'd found a way to merge her past with her present, just as Rory had said.

Rory.

Prior to her arrival in Lake Shire, she'd done little else but cry. Her aunt hadn't been able to reach her. Her cousins hadn't been able to reach her. Her friends hadn't been able to reach her. And after ten and a half months, she'd been tired of them trying.

So she'd packed what she could fit into her car and had taken off for Michigan, to the quiet and solitude of her uncle's inn. Within days she'd made progress, eating, smiling, laughing, dreaming….

And it was all because of Rory. He hadn't pushed. He hadn't insisted. He hadn't bribed. He was simply there. Listening when she spoke, talking when she needed to listen and guiding her along a path she needed to take.

Natalie's Nook wouldn't exist if it weren't for him. Sure, the desire was buried somewhere deep in her soul, but without Rory she doubted whether she'd have ever unearthed it.

His patience and his gentle encouragement had been the push she needed to keep busy. And as he'd predicted, forging a life didn't mean she had to forget.

Natalie's Nook was proof of that.

Maggie peeked out the window at the shoppers who were hurrying home to have dinner with their loved ones. This was the part that was hard. The part where her craft business fell short.

Sure, running the gift shop would keep her busy, giving her a reason to get out of bed every morning. But once five o'clock rolled around, there was nothing to guide her through the rest of the day. Nothing except loneliness.

And this persistent headache.

The headache. Maybe soft music would help. It certainly had when she was pregnant with Nat—

Maggie slapped a hand over her mouth.

Could it be?

"No, no, no," she whispered, as her feet automatically took her to her purse and the calendar she always carried.

It couldn't be. There was no way. They'd been together only once.

She stared down at the previous month's page, her stomach beginning to churn. The little red notation she'd faithfully used to track her cycle had ceased being needed eleven and a half months earlier.

Until now.

Suddenly the headaches made sense. So did the dizziness. The nausea was a little early, but it happened…

And so did coincidences.

Stress could affect a woman's cycle. Lack of sleep could cause headaches and dizziness. In fact, there were tons of reasons that could explain how she was feeling. There had to be.

Chapter Twenty

He heard her come in, the sound of her quiet footsteps in the hallway making his body react with longing. There were so many things he wanted to say to her, so many things he wanted to ask. Yet he stayed silent, the words burning a hole in his heart.

All afternoon he'd thought of little else but Maggie. Not the fact that he'd finished another room, or that the renovations would be complete in little more than a week. And especially not that he'd be putting his house on the market the second Christmas was over.

No, the only thought that seemed to stick in his head was Maggie. Four weeks ago, she'd been devastated, each step she took quickly undone by guilt and sadness. Yet in those short four weeks she'd picked herself up and found her dream, grabbing hold of it and making it come true.

He was proud of her and he wanted to tell her so. Only she didn't want to talk to him. Not now. Not ever.

It was a reality that pained him in a way few things did. The loss of his parents had been awful, yet he was grateful for the time they'd had. The loss of Reardon had been almost more than Rory could take, yet he was healing. But losing Maggie? Well, that was like nothing he'd ever felt before.

It was like losing a part of himself.

The best part.

Suddenly, the work he'd dreamed of all his life didn't satisfy him the way it had in the beginning. The truth behind the quiet life he'd come to accept was impossible to ignore. And the future he'd always been able to envision was suddenly more than a little murky.

In fact, the only thing that was clear these days was the hurt—the hurt and the fact that it wasn't going to change as long as she was within arm's reach.

Minnesota seemed as good a place as any to start over. Especially when he'd spotted the ad seeking restoration specialists. The change in geography would force him to snap out of the funk he'd been living in the past few weeks.

Yeah, it was time to take the advice he'd given Maggie at the beginning. A fresh start would do wonders. It had to.

Unhooking his tool belt from his waist, Rory dropped it into the box he kept in whatever room he was working on at the time. His stomach had started gurgling shortly after noon and he simply couldn't ignore it any longer.

He strode out the door and down the hallway, his feet instinctively taking the route that would keep him from getting too close to Maggie's suite. But four steps later he stopped.

Sure, there was a part of him that knew he should keep walking, knew that his knock would be unwelcome. But there was also a part—a louder part—that said he had to try.

Not because things would be any different. But because he simply wanted to tell her he was proud of her...

Before he said goodbye.

THE LINE WAS FAINT but it was there. Just as it was on the second and third tests she took for good measure.

She was pregnant.

"Pregnant," she whispered as she continued to stare at the pink line. "Pregnant."

Maggie remembered the moment she'd realized she was carrying Natalie, remembered the disbelief and the utter joy that had flooded her. Suddenly her mind had been consumed with images of cradles and diapers, teddy bears and blocks, mobiles and baby rattles.

It was the same exact feeling she had now.

"I'm carrying Rory's baby." She waited for the words to stir up fear, to dissolve her into tears as she would have imagined, but they didn't. Instead, they gave her hope. Hope for a life that had been cut short on an icy road in January.

The life she'd wanted to lead as Natalie's mother...

A life she would now lead with Natalie's half sibling.

Feeling the tears begin to flow, Maggie clutched the pregnancy test to her chest in much the same way she had Natalie's ornament four weeks earlier. Only this time, instead of longing for the past, she felt an unfamiliar pull in a direction she'd refused to consider until that moment.

For just as the shop had been a way to merge her past with her present, this baby—this precious life—would be a way to merge her past with her future.

SUMMONING UP EVERY OUNCE of courage he could find, Rory turned and headed toward Maggie's suite, the notion of seeing her face giving his feet the lift they needed. Even if she told him to leave, he'd still have gotten to see her one last time.

And if she didn't answer…well, he wasn't ready to entertain that thought. Not yet, anyway.

He lifted his fist to knock and then stopped, hearing an all too familiar sound wafting through the gap beneath the door.

Maggie was crying. Again.

Only this time they weren't the gut-wrenching sobs that had torn at him that first week. No, this time they were softer.

But just as they had in the beginning, they twisted his heart, pulled at the innate desire he had to fix things.

Only Maggie didn't want him to fix her. He'd tried. And she'd pushed him away. Again and again.

Who cared if he was proud of her? His telling her that wouldn't change anything. And as for goodbye, hadn't they said that already? The fact that he was going to Minnesota was nothing more than geography, wasn't it?

Slowly he turned away, jamming his hands into his pockets as he did. It was time to hang it up once and for all. Maggie was perfectly capable of fixing herself. It was time he concentrated on his own life.

Problem was, he was fairly certain a hammer and nails were no fix for a broken heart.

SHE DIDN'T KNOW HOW LONG she sat there, her back pressed against the wall, the pregnancy test still clutched in her hand. But it had been a while. The darkness that had descended on the room told that story.

But for once the tears hadn't been the kind that zapped her energy. No, this time they were different.

She was different. And she had to tell him the news.

Blowing a strand of hair from her forehead, she smiled when it returned to the same spot, oblivious of her efforts.

Few things had made her happy over the past eleven and a half months. In fact, if she thought about it, she could remember the things that had.

Beef stew.

Craft-supply shopping.

Caramel pie.

Belgian waffles.

And Rory.

It was the last one, though, that had been the reason behind all the others. And just like those instances, he was the reason behind the smile she hadn't stopped beaming since the pink line appeared—a smile she'd maintained even while the tears fell.

Her mind made up, she tucked the test into the front pocket of her jeans and turned the doorknob, her ears straining for any indication of Rory's presence in the inn. But there was nothing.

Not the tap of a hammer, not the whir of a power screwdriver, not the sound of his whistled songs. In fact, the hallway and all the rooms off it were dark.

Stepping back inside the suite, she walked to the window that overlooked the parking lot and saw that her car was the only vehicle present. She felt her shoulders slump for a split second before a new idea formed.

An even better one…

IT WAS NEARLY TEN O'CLOCK when she pulled up outside his home, the strip of light visible through the curtained front window allaying any fears he might be asleep. Things had taken longer than she'd hoped, thanks to a digital camera with batteries that needed replacing and an outfit that needed to be pressed.

But finally she'd finished.

Staring up at the house, Maggie felt the first pang of unease. What if he was fed up with her constant pushing and told her to take a hike? What if he didn't even want to hear her out?

He will. He loves you.

For weeks now Jack's voice had been guiding her steps, encouraging her to give Rory a chance. She'd resisted the sentiment with everything she had, refusing to acknowledge the fact that it was Jack's voice every bit as much as it was her own. But now she understood.

Rory made her happy. And Jack, of all people, would want her to be happy. It didn't mean she'd forget him.

How could she? Jack had taught her how to love, and he'd given her one of the greatest gifts of all.

But Rory had taught her things, too. He'd taught her to dream. He'd taught her to reach. He'd taught her that third chances were not only possible but worth fighting for. And he, too, had given her one of life's greatest gifts.

She ran a hand across her flat stomach and smiled. It was time.

HE GLANCED FROM THE DOOR to the clock and back again, irritation welling up inside his chest. What could anyone possibly want this late at night? Lifting the remote into the air, he increased the volume of the mindless drivel he'd managed to fall asleep to thirty minutes ago.

The knock came again.

Groaning, he tossed the remote onto the coffee table and rolled to his feet. "Who is it?" he snapped as he made his way over to the door, his bare feet making creaking sounds on the wood planked floor.

"It's me, Rory. It's Maggie."

He stopped in his tracks, his heart thudding.

"Please. I n-need to talk to you. But it's r-really c-cold out here."

Flinging open the door, he reached for her arm and pulled her inside. "What are you doing here?" The second the words were out, he tried to recall them. "Wait. I don't mean that the way it sounds. It's just that it's ten o'clock on the coldest night of the year."

Her teeth chattered as he ushered her into the hearth room toward the dwindling fire. Grabbing a log from the bin, he tossed it onto the grate and stoked the embers to life. "There you go. That should help."

"Thank you." She turned to him, and he saw that the tip of her nose was almost as red as the sweater peeking out at the neckline of her coat. "I'm sorry to bother you so late…but we need to talk and I'm hoping you'll say okay."

"Okay?"

"To talking. I was absolutely horrible to you the last time I was here, and I can only imagine how unhappy you must be to see me right now."

He stepped back, his eyes registering every detail of Maggie's presence, from the soft brown hair that cascaded down her spine to the black, knee-high boots that hugged her shapely legs in an alluring fashion. "Unhappy isn't the word I'd have chosen."

Her face fell. "I'm sorry, Rory. I really am. But because you are the way you are, it makes this whole thing more scary."

"Help me understand."

"Losing my parents as a little girl was awful. And losing Jack and Natalie nearly destroyed me. But you brought me back. To a place of joy. But if I lost you, too…" She stopped, took a moment to steady her voice. "Well, I'm not sure I could survive that. I'm not certain my heart could recover ever again."

"Your heart?"

She nodded. "I felt something for you that I tried to rationalize away as being anything but what it was. And the few times I thought maybe… Well, then I thought about what's happened every time I've felt safe and loved." Her voice grew hushed as her gaze locked with his. "And you…you must be so mad at me, mad that I just showed up like this."

He shook his head. "Hey…I'm not mad about you being here. I'm…I'm ecstatic." He grabbed hold of her hand and led her toward the couch. "But I'm a little confused, too. The last time you were here you made it pretty clear you didn't want to see me again."

"Because I couldn't."

"Couldn't?"

She wiggled out of her coat to reveal the soft curves of her body beneath a Christmas red sweater. "What happened that night happened because I wanted it to. And it felt right."

He sucked in his breath. "Then I don't understand. Why did you shut down on me?"

"Because I was scared."

Biting back the urge to speak, he simply waited, knowing that whatever had brought her to him would eventually reveal itself. The fact that she was there, within arm's reach, was all he needed at that moment.

"Having the kind of feelings I have for you opens a person up for unimaginable hurt. But so, too, does turning your back on it."

"Feelings?" he repeated. "You have feelings for me?"

The touch of her hand on his face told him everything he needed to know, though her words were just as powerful. "I've had feelings for you from the moment you first showed up on my doorstep. I tried to rationalize it away, tried to call it a million different things other than what it was, but at some point you have to see the truth. And the truth—for me—is that I care very deeply for you."

"Are…are you sure?"

The nod of her head nearly brought him to his knees. "Since the accident, everyone has been trying to get me to live again. And I resisted all of them. Yet something about you was different. You found things out about me—about my dreams and my wants—that I didn't even know myself anymore. You discovered them without pushing."

He couldn't help but laugh. "Siccing a personal knitting instructor on you wasn't pushing?"

"No."

"Dropping off a carton of craft supplies wasn't pushing?"

She shook her head.

"Dragging you through a shop that was going out of business wasn't pushing?"

She opened her mouth, only to close it in favor of a smile that brought his body to full attention.

He scooted closer to her on the sofa, her sheer presence making his head spin. "Then if it wasn't pushing, what was it?"

"Guiding, helping, believing, motivating…take your pick."

Grasping her hands in his, he caressed them with his thumbs, the feel of her skin driving him crazy. "You didn't mention the one I would have chosen."

She stared up at him. "Which one is that?"

"Loving."

She gasped. "Loving?"

"Loving," he repeated, his voice raspy with emotion. "Aw, Maggie, I've been miserable without you the past few weeks. It's like this ray of sunshine came into my life and cast my world in the most brilliant color it's ever known, only to have a cloud whip across the sky and blot it out again."

"I'm sorry. But you have to know that you've been on my mind, too. And slowly but surely, I've come to realize that denying the undeniable is no better…no easier than losing a part of yourself. Besides, loving you doesn't mean you're going to disappear from my life on an icy road just because it happened before. In fact, loving you is meant to be."

He nuzzled her forehead with his chin, her sweet scent seeping into every fiber of his being. "Meant to be?"

"Meant to be," she whispered, before leaning forward and extracting a familiar brown book from inside her bag. "Here."

"You've done more pages?" he asked in a gentle voice.

She nodded.

"May I see?"

Again she nodded, her gaze still locked on his.

He flipped open the book, noting each new page she'd added. One by one, he was treated to the memories that had shaped the woman seated beside him, memories he could now share thanks to the pictures and experiences she'd selected. When he got to the page she'd denoted as Natalie's Only Christmas, he looked up to find the expression in her eyes unreadable. "I'm so sorry, Maggie."

"Flip it over," she whispered as a lone tear ran down her cheek. "There's one more."

He did as he was told, confusion enveloping him as he looked at the next page. "What's this?"

"A new beginning."

"A new…" His mouth dropped open as his attention moved from the picture of the pregnancy test to the date written underneath.

"That's today's date," she stated.

"Today's date," he repeated, as his eyes sought to confirm her words. He sucked in his breath. "Is this real? I mean really, truly real?"

"As real as real can get."

Pushing the journal off his lap, he grabbed her face in his hands, his thumbs catching the tears that streaked her cheeks. "You're pregnant?"

"*We're* pregnant."

Chapter Twenty-One

Maggie listened to the soft sigh of his breath beneath her ear as he slept. Her face was pillowed by his muscular chest, her body protected by his powerful arms. Any reservations she'd had about his reaction to the pregnancy had vanished the second she'd told him. His whoops of joy had been nearly loud enough to wake the neighborhood.

But it was the part *after* that told her everything she needed to know. The part where he simply held her while the second most beautiful smile she'd ever seen stretched across his face.

Wiggling out of his arms, Maggie quietly slipped out of bed and made her way downstairs, where the twinkling lights of the Christmas tree guided her into the hearth room. For weeks she'd resisted the notion of Christmas, convinced it could never be as special as the one before. Yet the powers that be had shown her differently. What was special and wonderful about her past would remain special and wonderful in her memories. They were gifts she'd unwrap and treasure for as long as she could.

Now, there were new gifts to unwrap, like surprises

waiting to be unleashed. And just like before, she had someone to open them with. The face might be different, the relationship might be new, but love and hope linked them together.

"There you are."

She turned at the sound of his voice, a smile instinctively tugging the corners of her mouth upward.

"I was worried when I didn't feel you next to me."

Maggie stepped into Rory's arms when he approached, the warmth she found there bringing a mist to her eyes. "From the moment I moved into my uncle's suite, I saw my Christmas tree as a reminder of what wasn't. Yet here in your home, I see your tree as a symbol of what might be." Turning in his arms so her back was to his chest, she looked up at the tree, at the childhood ornaments he'd pointed out the night she'd come to dinner. "The way you've decorated it is like looking through a photo album—watching the progression of a life. And for some reason I find a comfort in that, one I haven't been able to find in a long time."

Tightening his arms around her, he rubbed his chin across the top of her head. "It won't be long before our little one has a handprint hanging from that tree, too."

Oh, how she hoped he was right. But Maggie knew there were no guarantees. Only hope.

As if reading her thoughts, he turned her to him once again, tilting her chin upward until they made eye contact. "We've both learned a thing or two about the precariousness of life. That alone will make us treasure every single second even more."

She rose up on tiptoe and brushed a kiss across his lips. "I love you, Rory."

"Oh, Maggie, I love you, too." Grabbing hold of her hand, he led her to the sofa they'd sat on earlier. "Looking at the tree just now reminded me of something."

"What's that?" she asked, as she settled into the crook of his arm.

"I want to hear all about Natalie's Nook."

She looked up at him, the tenderness in his eyes blanketing her heart with happiness. "You know?"

He nodded. "Delilah drove me by the shop today." He glanced at the clock on the DVD player, noted the early morning hour. "I mean, yesterday."

"And you didn't stop in?"

"I didn't think you'd want me to."

"I'm sorry, Rory. For everything."

"Don't be." He touched her face with the side of his hand and stroked it ever so gently. "You needed to learn to walk on your own before you were ready to trust someone else."

She considered his words. "I—I think you're right. But how? How did you know that?"

"I didn't. Delilah did."

Ahhh. Delilah. "I like her. A lot. She's a very special person."

"Agreed."

"Do you know that she talked Iris into letting me lease the building rather than buy it, enabling me to get in and open up before the holiday?"

He squeezed her tight. "I didn't know she had a hand in it. But I'm not surprised."

"The whole process has been like nothing I ever imagined." Maggie snuggled still closer, relishing the beat of his heart against her back. "And when that first customer walked in…well, it was…I don't know. I'm not sure I can even describe it."

"A dream come true?"

A dream come true.

"Yes. Like a dream come true. Only I'd stuffed it so far inside my heart I didn't even know it was still there." She swiveled around to face him. "But you…you not only uncovered it, you gave it wings."

He shook his head. "You gave it the wings, Maggie, not me."

She thought about that for a moment. "All right. Maybe I'm the one who flew…but I'm not sure I would have realized my wings were there if you hadn't pointed them out."

"I like looking at your wings," he teased, before covering her lips with his own.

Snaking her arms around his neck, she molded her body to his, the tenderness and strength she found there rocking her world for the umpteenth time. "Coming to Lake Shire was the smartest thing I've done in a long time," she said as their lips parted. "It gave me the shop, it gave me Delilah as a friend, it gave me clarity about my past and how it will always be present in my heart, it gave me you." She touched her stomach. "And it gave me—gave *us*—a new beginning."

"Lake Shire didn't give you those things."

"It didn't?" She planted a trail of kisses up the side of his face. "Are you sure?"

"I'm sure." His voice, husky with desire, made her body tingle in all the places he'd satisfied less than an hour earlier.

"Then who did?"

"Your uncle."

She pulled back to study Rory's face. "My *uncle?*"

"Well, technically, yes. Though I tend to put it more on his gift."

"Ahhh, the wishing ball." She thought back over the things she'd listed and the wishes the ornament had spawned. "Okay, I'll concede that his gift got the notion of wishes going. And I'll even concede that those wishes helped guide me toward the clarity I needed, but—"

"And they got you crafting again," he reminded her. "Which led to the store…"

"True. But I can't really say it brought me you or the baby. Not from a wish standpoint, anyway."

"Who said you were the only one allowed to make a wish?"

The teasing lilt to his voice, coupled with the lopsided grin that called his dimples into action, sucked her right in. "I'm sorry?"

"You did lend me the wishing ball for a few days, remember?" Rory pulled his hand from her face and gestured toward a bare spot in the center of the tree. "In fact, it hung right there, if you'll recall."

She followed the path of his finger. "I remember."

"If you think about it, you might also recall the fact that *I* actually filled out one of the slips it came with, and put it inside for safekeeping."

She looked back in his direction, his words pulling at

her heartstrings and sending her curiosity into overdrive. "And?"

"And what?"

She made a face at him. "And what was the wish?"

"I'd rather save that until you can read it with your own two eyes."

Shrugging, she grabbed her purse off the floor and stood. "If you say so. But I'll need to stand by the tree so I can read the words. It is kind of dark in here."

He jumped to his feet beside her and captured her hand before she could reach into her purse. "You brought it?"

"I did. In fact, I've had it in my purse to give back to you since…" she stared up at him "…since our child was conceived."

With his hand still on hers, she extracted the wishing ball that had put them in each other's path, forever changing their lives as a result. She held it up for him to see. "It really is beautiful, isn't it?"

His gaze left the ornament to focus on her, and she saw the tree's lights reflected in his eyes. "Yes, it is. In fact, she's the most beautiful thing I've ever seen."

"We're talking about the wishing ball, remember?" Maggie prompted.

"You might be, but I'm not."

She felt her face warm. "May I?" she whispered. Cocking her head toward the wishing ball, she waited for his permission.

Without saying a word he took the ornament from her hand and opened it, revealing its red velvet interior. Slowly, she took the small slip of white paper it held and unfolded it, her attention moving from it to Rory and back again.

She stared down at his bold handwriting, which stretched across the white surface like a shooting star across a night sky.

I wish for Maggie to find hope. With me. And in me.

"Hope," she repeated in a broken whisper. "Hope."

Wrapping his arms around her, he pulled her close once again, bringing tears to her eyes. "Have you found it?"

"Are you standing here next to me?" she asked.

His eyebrows furrowed. "Yes…"

"Is our child growing inside me?"

Reality dawned in his answering smile. "Yes."

"Then yes, Rory, I've found hope."

Epilogue

Twenty-One Months Later

She peeled the piece of tape off Delilah's outstretched hand and positioned it across the last of the streamers that traversed the dining-room ceiling. "How does it look?" she asked from her spot on the ladder. "Do you think it looks good?"

Delilah's face lit up. "With your eye for style and decorating? How could it not?"

Step by step Maggie descended the ladder, studying the room closely. "It's one thing to slap glue on a wooden picture frame or to create a centerpiece of candles, but it's quite another to pull off a first birthday party."

"You make them all look easy." Delilah crossed the room, her weathered hand gliding along the table Maggie had decked out in what could best be described as early Elmo. "She's going to love it."

"I hope so. But it might be hard to tell, since she smiles 24/7 anyway." And it was true. In fact, despite what the baby books claimed, she and Rory were convinced their precious angel had made her arrival with a smile planted on her face.

"That is true." Delilah led the way into the hearth room, stopping to tighten down one of the half-dozen balloons they'd tied around the space. "How is she holding up at the shop now that she's taking steps? Is it getting harder to have her there when you work?"

Maggie stopped beside the mantel, her eyes drawn to the picture of the birthday girl, her soft brown hair a mirror image of her half sister's. Even their noses favored one another. But her eyes? That ocean-blue color belonged to no one but her daddy. "She's doing great. It helps that I'm there only two days a week…but even on those days, her presence is a joy."

"I have it on good authority you're not the only one who feels that way."

Pulling her focus from the assortment of pictures that dotted the pine shelf, Maggie fixed it, instead, on the woman who had come to mean as much to their daughter as she did to her and Rory. "What are you talking about?"

"Just the other day, at the diner, a smattering of women came into the diner raving about Natalie's Nook. They talked about the hand-painted shelves, the seasonal hooks, the frames, the hand-painted window boxes, you name it. But they also talked about the baby. How she was the most precious thing they'd ever seen."

Maggie couldn't help but grin. "I wish they could have met."

"They?"

"My girls." Looking back at the mantel, she drank in the picture of Natalie she'd taken at the zoo nearly three years earlier. The similarities between the babies were striking at times, while in other ways they were different. And it was in those differences that she was reminded of the blessing she'd been given by having both Jack and Rory in her life.

Rory.

Drawing her thoughts back to the present, she glanced at her wrist. "Where are they? We've got a party to throw."

"Knowing Rory, he got caught up in showing his daughter to everyone in the park." Delilah crossed to the window and peered out at the road. "You know how he is."

And she did. Rory was amazing—as a father *and* a husband.

Smiling to herself, Maggie took a step to her left, reaching for the silver ball that had started it all—a wishing ball that sat in a place of honor on the mantel twelve months out of the year.

Footsteps in the hallway made her turn. "Rory, is that you?"

When he didn't answer, she peeked around the corner, the sight of her husband holding their sleeping child bringing tears of joy to her eyes. "She's *sleeping?*" she whispered.

"Like a baby."

He shifted their daughter to his other shoulder, then leaned forward to plant a kiss on Maggie's lips. "We can wake her in a few minutes. In the meantime, I can kiss you in private."

Delilah stopped midstep, cleared her throat and then spun around. "I'll go check on the cake now...make sure

Doug hasn't decided to have a piece before the party starts."

"Oh, hey, I didn't see you there," Rory rushed to explain. "I just got caught up in my wife, here."

"I remember what it was like to be young," she called over her shoulder. "So have your quiet smooch and call me when you're done."

Maggie watched as their friend disappeared into the kitchen, then looked back at Rory, the news she'd been holding in all morning begging to be shared. "I have something for you."

"You do?" he echoed, his voice light. "Shouldn't we wait until tonight for that?"

She rolled her eyes skyward. "Well, of course we'll wait until tonight for that…but that's not the something I'm talking about."

The baby shifted in her sleep, prompted, no doubt, by Rory's laugh. His eyes rounded as his hand went into automatic back-patting mode. "Can it wait? I think the birthday girl might be ready to party soon."

"It'll only take a moment." Maggie scurried into the hearth room, only to return to the hallway with the wishing ball in her hand. Holding it in his direction, she stared up at her husband. "Last time this helped us out. But this time I think we need to consult a book."

"A book?"

She nodded, her gaze never leaving his. "Uh-huh."

"What kind of book?"

"This kind." She reached into the hall closet and pulled out the paperback she'd purchased just that morning. Its title made the subject matter obvious.

He looked down at the volume, and his dimples flashed as he gave a smile that lit up her world. "Are you sure?"

Again she nodded.

Before he could say another word, the baby popped her head up. "Ahhh-bahh."

"Hello, there, sweet pea. Did you have a good rest on Daddy?" Maggie reached toward the baby and plucked her from Rory's arms. "Mmm, you smell so good, little one."

Rory stepped forward, the feel of his arms around them like nothing she could ever describe. "It may not be able to help with the name this time, but it sure has a knack for granting wishes."

"Granting wishes?"

He nodded.

"What are you talking about?" she asked, confusion knitting her brows.

"We're having another baby, right?"

"Yes."

With his eyes still fixed on hers, Rory opened the wishing ball and held it up for her to see a lone slip of paper against the red velvet interior. "Then it granted another wish."

"Ahhh-bahh!!"

Maggie blinked against the familiar sting of tears—a sensation that came because of joy these days rather than sorrow. "I think it's time, don't you?"

Rory nodded. "I agree."

"Are you ready?"

"I'm ready."

"Should we wait for Delilah?" She looked from Rory to the baby and back again, her happiness so complete it was almost too good to be true.

But it was true. As true as true could get.

He shook his head. "Nah. We'll just do an encore with her later. This one is for us."

"Okay, us it is." She shifted the baby in her arms so they could both see her face. "Ready?"

"Ready," he echoed.

"One…two…three…"

Their voices melded as their favorite smile of all brightened the space between them. "Happy birthday, Hope."

* * * * *

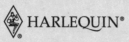

HARLEQUIN®

COMING NEXT MONTH

Available December 7, 2010

REQUEST YOUR FREE BOOKS!
2 FREE NOVELS PLUS 2 FREE GIFTS!

HARLEQUIN®

American ★ Romance®

Love, Home & Happiness!

YES! Please send me 2 FREE Harlequin® American Romance® novels and my 2 FREE gifts (gifts are worth about $10). After receiving them, if I don't wish to receive any more books, I can return the shipping statement marked "cancel." If I don't cancel, I will receive 4 brand-new novels every month and be billed just $4.24 per book in the U.S. or $4.99 per book in Canada. That's a saving of at least 15% off the cover price! It's quite a bargain! Shipping and handling is just 50¢ per book.* I understand that accepting the 2 free books and gifts places me under no obligation to buy anything. I can always return a shipment and cancel at any time. Even if I never buy another book from Harlequin, the two free books and gifts are mine to keep forever.

154/354 HDN E5LG

Name _____ (PLEASE PRINT)

Address _____ Apt. #

City _____ State/Prov. _____ Zip/Postal Code

Signature (if under 18, a parent or guardian must sign)

Mail to the **Harlequin Reader Service:**
IN U.S.A.: P.O. Box 1867, Buffalo, NY 14240-1867
IN CANADA: P.O. Box 609, Fort Erie, Ontario L2A 5X3

Not valid for current subscribers to Harlequin® American Romance® books.

Want to try two free books from another line?
Call 1-800-873-8635 or visit www.morefreebooks.com.

* Terms and prices subject to change without notice. Prices do not include applicable taxes. N.Y. residents add applicable sales tax. Canadian residents will be charged applicable provincial taxes and GST. Offer not valid in Quebec. This offer is limited to one order per household. All orders subject to approval. Credit or debit balances in a customer's account(s) may be offset by any other outstanding balance owed by or to the customer. Please allow 4 to 6 weeks for delivery. Offer available while quantities last.

Your Privacy: Harlequin is committed to protecting your privacy. Our Privacy Policy is available online at www.eHarlequin.com or upon request from the Reader Service. From time to time we make our lists of customers available to reputable third parties who may have a product or service of interest to you. If you would prefer we not share your name and address, please check here. ☐

Help us get it right—We strive for accurate, respectful and relevant communications. To clarify or modify your communication preferences, visit us at www.ReaderService.com/consumerchoice.

HAR10R

*See below for a sneak peek from our classic
Harlequin® Romance® line.*

Introducing DADDY BY CHRISTMAS by Patricia Thayer.

MIA caught sight of Jarrett when he walked into the open lobby. It was hard not to notice the man. In a charcoal business suit with a crisp white shirt and striped tie covered by a dark trench coat, he looked more Wall Street than small-town Colorado.

Mia couldn't blame him for keeping his distance. He was probably tired of taking care of her.

Besides, why would a man like Jarrett McKane be interested in her? Why would he want to take on a woman expecting a baby? Yet he'd done so many things for her. He'd been there when she'd needed him most. How could she not care about a man like that?

Heart pounding in her ears, she walked up behind him. Jarrett turned to face her. "Did you get enough sleep last night?"

"Yes, thanks to you," she said, wondering if he'd thought about their kiss. Her gaze went to his mouth, then she quickly glanced away. "And thank you for not bringing up my meltdown."

Jarrett couldn't stop looking at Mia. Blue was definitely her color, bringing out the richness of her eyes.

"What meltdown?" he said, trying hard to focus on what she was saying. "You were just exhausted from lack of sleep and worried about your baby."

He couldn't help remembering how, during the night, he'd kept going in to watch her sleep. How strange was that? "I hope you got enough rest."

She nodded. "Plenty. And you're a good neighbor for

coming to my rescue."

He tensed. Neighbor? *What neighbor kisses you like I did?* "That's me, just the full-service landlord," he said, trying to keep the sarcasm out of his voice. He started to leave, but she put her hand on his arm.

"Jarrett, what I meant was you went beyond helping me." Her eyes searched his face. "I've asked far too much of you."

"Did you hear me complain?"

She shook her head. "You should. I feel like I've taken advantage."

"Like I said, I haven't minded."

"And I'm grateful for everything…"

Grasping her hand on his arm, Jarrett leaned forward. The memory of last night's kiss had him aching for another. "I didn't do it for your gratitude, Mia."

Gorgeous tycoon Jarrett McKane has never believed in Christmas—but he can't help being drawn to soon-to-be-mom Mia Saunders! Christmases past were spent alone…and now Jarrett may just have a fairy-tale ending for all his Christmases future!

Available December 2010, only from Harlequin® Romance®.

HREXP1210

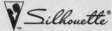

ROMANTIC
SUSPENSE

Sparked by Danger, Fueled by Passion.

RACHEL LEE
A Soldier's Redemption

When the Witness Protection Program fails at
keeping Cory Farland out of harm's way, ex-
marine Wade Kendrick steps in. As Cory's new
bodyguard, Wade has a plan for protecting her—
however falling in love was not part of his plan.

Conard County THE NEXT GENERATION

*Available in December
wherever books are sold.*

Visit Silhouette Books at www.eHarlequin.com

SRS27705